ONE OF TH

ONE OF THE FAMILY

Nora Brocas Sanderson

*A man, his wife, his axe, his tree,
and the beginnings of the family*

STEELE ROBERTS

Thanks to all the friends and family who have supported the publishing of Mum's Hokianga memories. She wrote them not as a solemn historical record but with a loving twinkle and a mischievous grin. May you enjoy them in the same spirit, and celebrate her memory with delight.

~ *Martyn Sanderson*

© Estate of Nora Sanderson 1999

Cover image – KAL; photo research – Marg Morrow; production assistance – Lynn Peck

Published in 1999 by Roger Steele
STEELE ROBERTS LTD, Box 9321 Wellington, Aotearoa New Zealand
Phone (04) 499 0044 – Fax (04) 499 0056
rwsteele@actrix.gen.nz • http://home.clear.net.nz/pages/srl/

1-877228-18-4

CONTENTS

I	Tapu Bush	7
II	Academic pursuits	13
III	Accident-prone	26
IV	Entertainment a go-go	35
V	Grist to our mill	41
VI	Manna in the desert	51
VII	Things that go bump	56
VIII	Farm for sale	60
IX	Is there a doctor…?	68
X	Thanksgiving vacation	79
XI	Shadow of the law	88
XII	Gentle Jesus	92
XIII	Noxious weed inspector	97
XIV	A small miracle	104
XV	Not without incident	111
XVI	Something will have to be done	117
XVII	Sunday afternoon walk	122
XVIII	Mop	129
XIX	Festive occasion	136
XX	Beyond our ken	143
XXI	Friends and neighbours	147

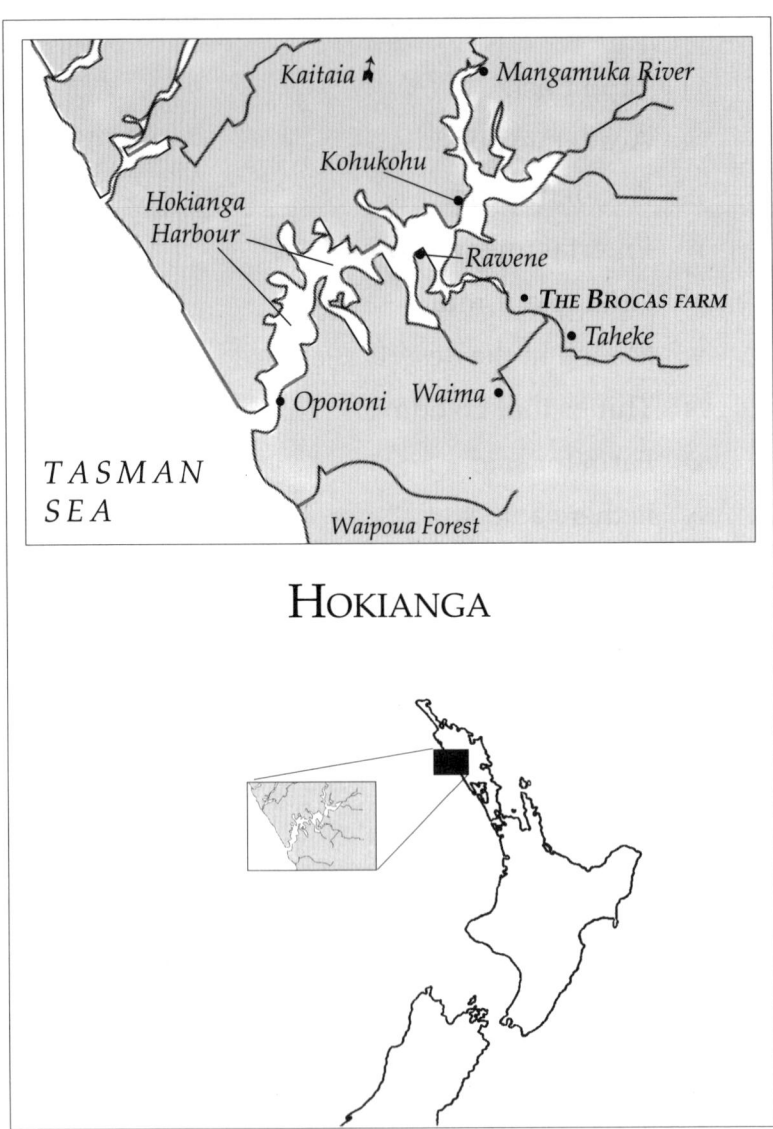

I

Tapu Bush

Our parents were deeply religious, and saw to it that all nine of us had a pretty good working knowledge of Heaven and Hell almost before we were out of our nappies. So when as a child I fell out of a top-storey window I already knew about God and was convinced it was up to Him to rescue me before I made violent landfall on the garden below, though why He tipped me out of the window in the first place remained a mystery to me. I was fairly sure He wouldn't do it on purpose even though my record for that day was a little smudged. I had sneaked my plate of porridge out to the cat instead of eating it myself.

My faith was not betrayed. It could be no mere coincidence that the garden had been dug over only the day before, and was loose-soiled and soft to land on. God had stretched out His hand to me in visible and tangible friendship, to save me from a broken neck. I generously decided to overlook the question, *did I fall or was I pushed?* As far as I was concerned, God had moved in. He was now one of the family.

Circumstances usually did work out so that His friendship remained unquestioned, but there were times… the Tapu Bush incident, for instance. Let me tell you about it.

That warm and sunny afternoon in the Hokianga we younger members of the family found ourselves bored almost to tears by the company of adult visitors. Our restlessness communicated itself to everyone else in the large but overcrowded living room. The neighbouring farmers and their wives were there to attend a service conducted by a visiting minister. Mother's custom was to invite the parishioners to stay to a midday meal, so there they were, well fed and conversational. Only we were bored.

"I think you children had better go out and play." Mother had at last got the message. We went gladly. This was better than being expected to sit passively in the corner all Sunday afternoon. The adults stopped talking to watch us file out of the room. We felt they would miss our bright presence. Still, be that upon Mother's head, she'd said go and that was what we were doing. We were in fact going much further than she had in mind.

For some time we youngsters had discussed paying a visit to the Tapu Bush, a reserve three or four miles up-river towards Taheke from Dad's farm. Today seemed a likely enough occasion, since no one would look for us until it came time to fetch the cows from the nearby Sunday paddock.

I'll admit I was not madly enthusiastic. Even the thought of setting foot upon the banks of the Tapu Bush reserve drained my courage. I was sure my brothers were scared too and would change their minds at the last minute, but it seemed I had been mistaken. Here we were, almost on our way.

Stories about the Tapu Bush were many and varied. Even in our time there was, we were told, a strong possibility of trespassers being caught, taken from the bush and held tapu for some days.

This had happened to a Pakeha, a white man, we were told by our Maori friends. This man was taken from the Tapu Bush by tohungas and confined to a whare, a Maori hut, for some days. With his hands fastened behind his back he was fed like a small child, or so the story goes, and at that time we saw no reason to disbelieve it.

The Maoris were not imposing punishment on the trespasser, they were merely carrying out an ancient custom. Any hands, Pakeha or Maori, having touched tapu material were reckoned to be unfit to handle food. Apart from the nuisance of being detained against his will the Pakeha in question was treated with courtesy and consideration, but our guess is that he was one scared white man busy making up his mind never to trespass on other folks' property again as long as he lived.

As an ancient burial ground, every inch of the Tapu Bush was sacred to the Maori. When we were living in the Hokianga, the Maori gathered together a priceless store of greenstone and this they committed to a cave in the Tapu Bush, knowing that no Maori worth his salt would ever touch that pounamu again, no matter if he were offered a king's ransom for the precious jade. For a white man to filch any of the store would be like robbing a grave and just as dishonourable an action. He would deserve any punishment he might get.

In any case no one could break through to the greenstone, the Maoris saw to that. They erected a monument, a sort of tombstone, over the mouth of the cave, sealing away the sacred jade for ever.

Not satisfied with glimpses of the monument as we passed up-river in Father's launch, we children would borrow the binoculars and scan the inscription more closely. Even at that early age we found it oddly jarring that the modern white stone was inscribed in the lower corner, So-and-So, Stonemasons, Auckland.

Anyway, there we were this Sunday afternoon, the four youngest members of our large family, mooring our boat to the big old cabbage tree which leaned out over the tidal waters of the river. As we made our way into the cool, dark, unutterably mysterious depths of the forest, I was not at all happy. I don't believe my brothers were exactly hilarious over the project either, now we were into the bush.

The air was heavy with the musty smell of decaying leaves underfoot. Even on that hot summer's day interlacing branches overhead dripped moisture down our necks. Vines offered their huge white-petalled lilies and for a moment we hesitated. Normally we would have eaten dozens of the fleshy, tangy petals, each three inches or more across the base. Mother enjoyed the petals too, and so did Father. Perhaps we should take some back to them?

But somehow we felt squeamish about eating anything grown in the Tapu Bush. After all, we wouldn't gather cabbages or any other food from our own sacred grounds. Not that cabbages would ever be lined up in a cemetery, but the meaning was there in our minds.

Besides, Father would take his leather belt to us if he ever found out we'd taken anything from the Maoris' Tapu Bush. He'd be sure to impress upon us that punishment would be immediately forthcoming in some form from God, but he'd feel bound to add his quota as well. He had a deep respect for Maori religious beliefs.

Near the bush track leading to the Waima Maori village there was a long, low mound, overgrown by native shrub and blackberry vines. We were told this was the grave of an ancient chief killed in a tribal battle. To the Maori this spot was sacred indeed. Father knew this and would have punished us severely had we taken even so much as a root of fern from there. We children were frightened of that mound. Not even the shrill merry music of the cicadas piping from the willow boughs overhead could brighten that sombre spot.

We were equally scared of setting foot in the Tapu Bush and for once were willing to admit it. We had felt a strange reluctance to scramble out of our rowing boat even after it was safely moored. The sharp whirr of some large bird's wings past our faces as we entered the bush didn't help much, either. Probably the ominous ruru, the morepork. Any Maori would warn us we'd be heading for some pretty bad luck if a ruru flew in our faces.

We were by now barefoot, our Sunday shoes discarded. Creepy, sludgy creatures slid away or squashed beneath our feet in the damp green moss. We doubted if human feet had ever before trod that moss. Bush-lawyer vines reached out jagged saw-like fingers and ripped our arms and legs. An outsize locust-like weta tangled itself deep into my hair. In my horror I couldn't decide whether it had leapt at me or merely fallen from the branches overhead.

I wanted to rush out of the bush and go home, but I knew I had a fat hope of getting the boys to listen to my whimperings. They had dedicated themselves to exploring the Tapu Bush and that is what they meant to do. I had the choice of going deeper into the bush with them or sitting alone in the boat. Since there was nothing I wanted less than to be alone I went along with them.

How we became separated I shall never know. I'm sure my brothers didn't deliberately ditch me — not in the Tapu Bush. They wouldn't be so heartless as to abandon even an animal there.

Being lost is a strange feeling. At first you think you'll catch up with the others any moment. Then you begin to panic and wonder if you will ever catch up with them. You laugh at yourself and think, gosh, I can find my way out, there's nothing to it. Fancy thinking I'm lost!

After five minutes or so of plunging ahead through dense forest which presents exactly the same face whichever way you look, you know you are going to die there. At this stage I took off, bawling blue murder, running and stumbling and taking a header over small precipices I didn't see in the dense undergrowth.

There was a large kiekie, its plush leaves a pale opalescent green with clusters of scarlet berries, growing high up the trunk of a leaning rata tree. It was quite some time before I realised I was passing the same tree every so often. I was going round in circles, just as some lost people are said to do.

There was neither sound nor sight of the boys anywhere. They must have gone on their way, penetrating deeper into the forest, imagining I was dawdling timidly along in the bush behind them. How they missed hearing the din I was kicking up goodness only knows; the density of the forest probably deadened the sounds of my anguish.

That was the most terrifying experience of my young life to date. I learned that it is quite true one's life parades before one's eyes. I recalled every sin I had ever committed — the times I'd stayed at the back of the farm making dolls' houses in the tall bracken fern when I knew it was time to go home and feed the calves with their midday ration of skim milk and shark oil. Or the time I missed my turn to dry the after-dinner dishes. Deliberately.

Not long ago I'd burned a new hair-ribbon under the copper and allowed Mother to believe I'd lost it somewhere out on the farm. Hair ribbons were so sissy, I hated them, but now I knew that was no excuse. And there was the night Mother said I could help myself to just one peppermint out of the big glass jar and I took two. She must have noticed my bulging cheeks and my haste to get out of the room. Lost now in the Tapu Bush I wished I might have been allowed to live long enough to tell Mother I was sorry.

With all this on my conscience I couldn't expect any help from God. Besides, He must have been extra busy on Sunday. I didn't feel I had the right to bother Him.

Suddenly, there was the river! I could hardly believe my eyes. The boys were sprawled on the bank picking blackberry thorns out of their feet.

"Took your time, didn't you?" they accused. "We've got to be getting out of here. Did you think we were staying the night?"

They really had not heard my bellowing. I swallowed rather painfully before I spoke. "Just thought I'd take a look through the bush a bit."

They gaped. "Golly! You've got your nerve about you, haven't you? Wouldn't catch me poking about the Tapu Bush by myself."

"It was fun," I boasted, Heaven forgive me!

We sneaked out into midstream and crept with exaggerated noiselessness down the river towards home. I was quite sure I heard laughter coming from somewhere along the riverbank. It was laughter!! Good-natured laughter.

Our trespassing was seen, but forgiven. No one ever told tales to our parents about our visit to their Tapu Bush, but we never went back. I hope their priceless greenstone lies there still, undisturbed.

Back home and with time to give the matter some thought, I felt God really had let me down rather badly. Those black moments alone in the Tapu Bush were not funny. I might not be perfect but all the same I didn't deserve to die of fright.

Granny was in the next room chatting with Mother. I forgot my own troubles for the moment, my attention caught by what Granny was saying. "They tell me Mrs Bly had her twelfth baby today, with God's help, the poor soul."

So that is where God was today. Fair enough, I excused Him. Mrs Bly's mysterious needs were probably greater than mine, lost and all though I was.

II

Academic pursuits

Father's very conservative English brother registered sheer horror when, on a visit to our farm in the Hokianga, he found us youngsters running about bare-footed.

We blamed him for the gumboots Father forced us into. We also blamed him for a leakage of information to the Education Department. If Uncle didn't tell them we (along with a dozen neighbouring children) were without a school, who did?

Whether or not Uncle sabotaged us, it was shortly after his visit that the education authorities became aware of our existence. The discovery seemed to startle them. They wrote excitedly to Father about us.

Father's answer was to clear out the small unlined building on the riverbank, once used as a grocery store for the millhands. There he installed our household help as teacher, complete with half-a-dozen desks and a sheaf of switchy, stinging supplejack canes cut from the nearby bush.

The arrangement seemed to work out not too badly, but after falling in the river twice and being nearly washed out the schoolroom door every time the river rose in flood, the lady gave up. When I started school we had a brand new teacher, young and very charming.

We were delighted to discover our new teacher's capacity for sleep, one of our pleasant duties being to wake her urgently when we caught sight or sound of the school inspector's launch drawing near the wharf beside the school. Since we were not likely to have it so good with a replacement teacher we made it our business to see she was wide awake and on the ball when the inspector walked in the door. We also made sure she had plenty of time to hide the large box of chocolates which normally occupied the place of honour on her table.

A great deal of our time was taken up with hopscotch which we played on the hard-baked clay yard outside the door, taking turns to keep an eye on the teacher and sound the alarm if she stirred or showed signs of lifting her pretty head.

As long as we filed dutifully into school in the morning and filed out again at three o'clock the day was practically our own. I think we probably did a little school work just for the look of it, timing our scholastic efforts for the intervals when Teacher was awake. She must have been a great girl for late-night parties.

We'd never had life so good. The hours of study which automatically exempted us from farm chores were in fact non-existent. We got away with murder. Father was much too busy to keep a check on our scholastic activities. Besides, he trusted us, poor man.

Imagine our dismay when Teacher announced she was leaving to get married. We hoped something drastic might overtake her fiancé but fate was against us. They were duly married and her place was taken by a stranger, a man, young and frighteningly competent. We saw at once we would have to begin learning or be left standing in the punishment corner for the rest of our lives.

Our days took on a dreadful monotony. Sums, spelling, writing. Spelling, writing, reading, lunch break. Battle of Hastings and Spanish Armada. And essays by the hundred. *"I saw a calf coming to school this morning." "I saw a big bunch of flax coming to school this morning." "I saw two of Father's plough horses coming to school this morning."* We wondered why the teacher developed a habit of sitting with his head in his hands.

He didn't last long. A baptism of flood waters he could take more-or-less philosophically. In the winter months he became quite expert at marshalling us all out of the school and onto higher ground minutes before swirling muddy river water took over the entire room. But fire and water combined, no. He packed up and left immediately after the fire in our school chimney.

It was a home-made chimney fashioned out of corrugated roofing iron, built wide and open to the sky. The first really cold morning ushering in the winter, we lit a bonny wood fire, but we forgot to allow for birds' nests and what-have-you, legacy of a long dry summer. With a great roar, the chimney set on fire.

Men came running from the nearby mill. Someone climbed onto the roof and covered the chimney opening with wet sacks. The fire died down, but Teacher was the worrying kind. He stuck his head into the chimney to make sure all sparks were out — and received several gallons of water over his face and head, muddy river water thickened with greasy black soot. Someone on the roof had also been worrying about stray sparks.

We heard Teacher muttering something about there being a limit to what any normal human being can take. He went, quite gladly we felt, to a teaching position in the Congo.

No one seemed eager to take over his job, so the school was closed. But our triumph was short-lived; the powers-that-be sprouted a school three miles away, down-river. Father went to look at the new school and came home incensed. What was so different about it? The building was small and square and unlined exactly as was our school. He forgot to mention that it was well above the level of the flood waters, which our own building certainly was not.

A heated argument sprang up between Father and the education people. Father said he had a legal case against our being forced to go to school. No child could be made to cross a wide and dangerous tidal river, much less be forced to row three miles to school in the morning and three miles home at night. The education people said never mind about all that, we had to be educated somehow, by hook or by crook. Their answer was for Father to take us to school and back in his launch.

Fine, Father agreed, if they would come and do his farm work while he was spending hours every day running about the countryside with a pack of children.

Their answering letter was pretty terse. Father came back at them with the news that his launch was laid up on the bank with a busted keel; he'd crashed into a sunken log at low tide. It wouldn't be in use for weeks, or months. Possibly even a year.

Three letters arrived from the Education Department by the next mail, each more emphatic than the last. Father took advice from a local lawyer. No, we could not be made to cross a deep tidal river. Fine. Father decided to go his own sweet way and ignore the authorities. They couldn't answer him back as long as he didn't write to them.

We continued to run wild, blissfully. Bare-footed young heathens. I think Mother probably worried a great deal about our threatened illiteracy, especially as she herself was intelligent and cultured, a fan of good literature.

There was, amazingly, no further word from Headquarters. It would seem Father had won the argument. But then he awoke to the horrifying idea that he might be stuck with a crowd of dependants rated at approximately Standard Two for the rest of their lives.

He set to work and rebuilt the holed wreck of a rowing boat lying on the riverbank. By the time he'd finished safeguarding our future with bits of board here and there and had built a new bottom into the old tub, he'd evolved a craft half as big as the Queen Mary. A great pontoon of a thing which should have had a whole galley of slaves to row it along.

Father meant well, but how we did hate that boat! The *Enterprise*, he christened her. I wonder we ever got to school in her at all. The old beast had a habit of sinking to the bottom of the river while we were in the classroom. All we could see when we came down to the school wharf would be a taut rope stretching to some object out of sight under the muddy water. At least we had the stout rope with which to drag the tub up onto the bank and drain out the water, but were those seats cold and wet and muddy to sit on!

The Battle of the Boat became a phobia with us. We hated her and were convinced she hated us, obstinate beast that she was. We could almost hear her chuckling as we battled against the current. We weren't chuckling. Hot and tired, we usually quarrelled like mad all the way home. We sometimes paused to wonder if God was listening to our squabbling but decided He'd understand our difficulties even though He'd probably never had to row a miserable old tub like the *Enterprise*, Himself.

Our teacher was a natty dresser. The afternoon she fell in the river she was wearing a peach-coloured linen suit with matching silk blouse. Very smart. We never knew how she came to miss her footing as she stepped into the boat. There was a splash, and next minute up came Teacher from the depths beside the boat in which I had been busily setting out the oars and rowlocks ready to start home.

I couldn't help — I knew she couldn't swim, but neither could I. She clung to the gunwale, gasping and beginning already to laugh at her own plight. From the wharf above us the boys shouted out excited instructions.

"Don't get on the same side of the boat, you'll swamp the whole thing!" "Give her the oar to hang onto!" And so on, while I dithered about the boat scared any move I made would make matters worse.

"Get out the oars and turn the boat! Back the teacher onto the mud and she can crawl out that way."

"Why not back her onto the wharf steps?"

"You can't. The tide'll swing your bow downstream and you'll drown her." The teacher took no part in the discussion.

Please, God, help me. I began to bawl. It would be horrible to see anyone drown, and besides I'd probably go to Mt Eden prison, for life. I had heard about manslaughter.

I got the oars out somehow and rowing with one oar while I back-pedalled with the other I managed to turn the boat, with Teacher clinging desperately, the jacket of her linen suit floating out behind her on the water. Her main concern seemed to be to keep her beret on.

I had to take her into the muddy bank carefully or she'd have ended up with the keel of the boat across her lap as she was forced into a sitting position. When she finally struggled up the greasy, oozing mudbank to firmer ground, there wasn't even a faint smile on anyone's face, though Heaven knows she looked funny enough to send us into hysterics. It was she who began to laugh. A great sport, indeed.

The oddest sight was that chic, expensive, coffee-coloured beret still clinging tenaciously to a head of straggling wet hair. We bet she couldn't dive in again and come up with her hat on in a hundred years.

I knew what it was like to fall into that river, I'd fallen in more than once and been fished out, hilariously, by my brothers. Dithering with one bare foot on the bank and the other on the bow of the boat, too scared to make a decisive move either back to the bank or into the boat, a header into the muddy water was unavoidable. I exonerate the boys from all blame. No one could keep a boat nosed into a greasy, slippery bank indefinitely. Before I'd made up my mind the boat would be drifting away from the shore and there wasn't much they could have done about it.

Or was there felonious intent? No, I refuse to entertain such an ungenerous suspicion. Besides, they would have nothing to gain by dunking me in the river. I accompanied them to school anyway, mud and wet clothes notwithstanding. They would have known they had no chance of getting rid of my irritating presence in the boat, and in any case there would have been one less to pull the oars in the heavy old tub.

Our greatest joy was to be given a tow home. The putt-putt-putt of an approaching launch was the sweetest sound anyone might hear, especially when the tide was running against us.

Most launchmen were extremely kind. They would slow the launch almost to a stop, we'd row like mad to bring our boat alongside, throw the launchman our line and when we were made fast we'd scramble on board and sit there on the launch seats feeling like Royalty.

Some of the launchmen let us stay in the boat being towed behind the launch at a good rate of knots. This was fun, too, though not really any more permissible than towing a family in a caravan behind a car. If Father happened to be near the wharf on these rare occasions he'd rush to the landing steps and blast off most ungratefully. "What are you doing? Trying to drown the children?"

No wonder old Bunny never stopped either to pick us up or tow us behind his small, squat, square-looking launch. He quite frequently passed us at speed. The wash from his launch would probably have sunk a lighter rowing boat, but our gigantic old tub merely wallowed slightly in an aloof and dignified manner.

If we were tired enough to sink our pride and call out to Bunny begging for a tow he'd stand up and shake his fist and proceed to give his version of our ancestry. My brothers kindly explained to me the meaning of some of the words but most of the epithets passed over our heads.

We never did find out why he hated us so violently. Perhaps he hated all children. Poor old Bunny. The story ran that he was in his younger days a jockey in Australia and was reputed to have ridden to victory a famous horse called Bundurra. Hence the name, Bunny. I think the story was true. He was small-boned and light enough to have been a jockey.

Oh, well. Bunny's lack of co-operation was made up to us by the unfailing kindness of the neighbouring Maoris. If they happened to be going our way they would draw alongside our boat, grab the tow line and take off, paddling their big canoe for dear life. We'd help by rowing with our own oars, setting a spanking pace between the lot of us.

Usually the Maori women did the paddling — the plump and good-natured wahine. The tane lolled at his ease in the stern of the canoe, as often as not sound asleep.

I felt when we passed these wahine paddling silently along, my brothers were making silent comparisons. How nice it would be for the three of them to loll back and lazily allow me to row them to school and home again. That was definitely not one of the penalties

Canoe races at Kohukohu

I was prepared to pay for being such a hoyden.

Someone who should have known better once took it upon herself to make mischief over my tomboyish habits. She invited me to visit her at her own home then chose the very moment when I was biting into a gorgeously ripe pear to put me in the witness box.

Having first completely mystified me by saying, "You can tell me the truth, dear. Whatever you say won't go any further," she asked me if I did indeed have something to tell her.

She seemed so hopeful I tried to come up with some interesting bit of news. After all, I owed it to her to be as obliging as possible, seeing that she'd fed me copiously on lamingtons, lemonade and ripe pears ever since I'd set foot in her house a couple of hours ago.

So I said, "Excuse me for having my big toe wrapped in bandages. I was going to tell you about it, anyway. Uncle says it's our own fault we suffer the agony of kicking our toe-nails off against the scoria rocks at our place. He says if we wore shoes…"

"No, no, dear! That's not what I want you to tell me about. Isn't there anything else you have on your mind?"

"Granny has a new set of take-out teeth," I was still game to keep on trying. There must be some item of news that would hold her interest? The obligation I was under weighed me down. Four pears, or five? And she'd let me play the gramophone, too. Edison records. The man's voice sounded strange, as though he was talking through his nose. Harry Lauder was good…

"Come on, dear!" she was becoming impatient. "You know what I want to hear, don't you?"

Feeling a bit of a fool I shook my head. But then I remembered. "We're getting a brand new bath up from Auckland. Father says we kids have rattled the guts out of the old bath…"

"You're just being deliberately more stupid than usual," she sounded cross. "You know all the time what I mean. Now, is it or is it not true that you spend every playtime at school and most of your lunch hour up in the forest with the Maori boys?"

She must have been staggered when I said of course it was true, I went off into the forest with the boys every chance I had.

She was looking strangely at me and seemed to have gone red in the face. "Don't you think you should have a nice little talk with your mother about this, dear?"

Puzzled, I said, "Mother knows. She said she doesn't mind me running wild a bit and having a good time while I'm young. She says, after all, school can be a bit boring if we haven't got any amusements…"

I thought she was going to faint. It was years before I realised what she was getting at. Pity my simplicity, indeed! And thank God for the wholesome, clean-minded mates we had at school.

We lost one of our Maori schoolmates. The trouble between him and the teacher arose over the question of cannibalism. The teacher happened to remark that there had never been cannibalism among the Maori tribes, or at least the practice had never been proved. Our young friend got to his feet in such a flurry he knocked his desk over. He was furiously insulted. Of course there had been cannibalism among the Maoris! He was a Maori himself, he should know. The teacher was talking through a hole in her head.

The teacher said not to be stupid, he wasn't telling the truth. What human being would eat the flesh of their fellow man?

He found a prompt answer to that question: his grandparents had eaten human flesh. Granted it was the flesh of a sworn enemy of their tribe, but enemy or not the victim was still human.

The teacher gazed at him in blue-eyed horror. "Would you eat human flesh? Not that I believe your story anyway…"

"No thank you, not for me," he winked briefly at my brothers and added, "They say it tastes horrible. Not enough salt, you see?"

I think the caning the teacher gave him was really meant to save her face. She must have heard the subdued giggling from the class. "You'll stay back after school and write a hundred times, *My ancestors did not eat human flesh*," she told the boy.

"I'll stay in at lunchtime and write it then," he suggested. He wrote a hundred times *My ancestors did eat human flesh*. By the time the teacher had discovered the crucial word was omitted he'd left the classroom — for good.

Mysterious airborne objects thudded onto the tin roof throughout the afternoon, coming unmistakably from the direction of the nearby hillside forest, but there was nothing the teacher could do about it. We knew she was in the wrong but we were all too gutless to stand up for the poor kid. His empty desk held for us an unspoken reproach. It was days before anyone thought to remove the half-eaten raw quince from the pencil-slot.

About this time we found ourselves quite out of the blue being whisked off to a city school with a roll of nine hundred pupils. We felt incredibly sissy, stepping into a warm and comfortable bus every morning almost at our door. The hated old *Enterprise* became somehow a symbol of our lost independence. We despised the soft city kids and were horrified to learn they hardly knew a calf from a foal and had never in their lives watched a genuine rough-riding rodeo, except perhaps on the movies.

I returned abruptly to laying my troubles at God's door. Why had He elected to spirit us off to the city? He must surely have known how we'd hate city life! I asked Him politely but with deepening urgency to please relent and dump us back at square one in the country.

Believe it or not we were whisked back to the Hokianga farm. I was fairly sure my pleadings would be answered but it was still a pleasant surprise to find ourselves at home again, and so soon. I gave all the credit to God, but no doubt Father had something to do with it. It was good to be back but we did feel that our few months in the city had not been entirely wasted. We'd at least learned to cross a busy street without having the car drivers lean out to curse us. In Rawene, our nearest village, there was only the one car, Dr Smith's choking, coughing Trojan, which fairly shook the whole township when the doctor ventured out behind the wheel. You'd have to be an absolute nutcase to get yourself caught beneath the wheels of a Trojan, but city cars were much more aggressive.

We'd also developed a highly civilised taste for ice cream and who-done-it movies. No, indeed, our time had not been wasted. One of the older boys at the city school had even gone to some trouble to teach us how to play housie. There was little in it for him, a mere handful of our carefully hoarded pocket money.

We did not take too kindly to returning to rowing ourselves to school and back every day, come Hell or high water. Or even flood-swollen waters. Our city-soft hands blistered badly when we first took up the oars again.

This town-country thing came into it, too. We were bitterly hurt when the kids at school called us townies and snubbed us unmercifully. They suggested we could go back and live in the city if we preferred city friends. It took some bleeding noses and one or two loosened teeth to convince them we had not altered much during our absence.

"Righto," the kids said, "now you're back, see if you can get rid of the new teacher. Should be easy, he's fat and lazy and hasn't got the brains of a hedgehog. He can't even row a boat!"

Getting rid of the teacher seemed a strange price to pay for their friendship but we decided to oblige. It wouldn't be too difficult a task anyway with quite a wide choice of ways and means offering.

We chose wasps. The teacher had unthinkingly asked to have a collection of honey-combed, brown-paper-like wasps' nests placed at his disposal. The dinner-plate size of the nests seemed to fascinate him.

We smoked the wasps out of the nests, gathered them in dozens from flax bushes and fence wires and filled his room during his absence over the weekend. I must confess we knew the grubs would hatch out in that hot room, ready to greet the teacher in their angry hundreds when he opened the door on Monday morning.

It worked. He left at the end of the week, but our understandable exuberance was slightly dampened by pangs of conscience. Our teacher was not a pleasant sight with both eyes almost closed, plus a swollen nose and every finger as fat as a pork sausage.

Still, he took with him a sugar sack of vacated wasp nests which we were sure would cause a gratifying sensation among his city friends. Especially if there happened to be a grub or two waiting to hatch out. We doubted if this would happen, the embryonic wasps were probably drowned anyway. The teacher almost missed the overnight ferry at Rawene and was in such a panic at the thought of spending another week with us he leapt aboard and dropped his suitcase into the water. It took two sailors and much bad language to rescue it.

Since no one else seemed willing to throw themself into the lions' den the Education Department was forced to close the school down. I don't know how the older children fared, but we younger ones had our education taken over by an elder sister. This suited us better than it suited her, especially as Father took the Heaven-sent opportunity of introducing Bible lessons into the schoolroom curriculum.

Poor Fay. Her orderly mind decreed that she begin at the beginning. She must have been astounded to learn how much there is to argue about in the Old Testament. Adam and Eve we knew about, and the Garden of Eden and all that. We even knew that the first quarrel began about an apple. With memories of a house-proud grandmother we assumed that Adam ate the apple and threw the core and skins on the polished floor. Or was it Eve who ate the apple? Adam probably thought she should have made it into an apple pie for his dinner.

We argued about these finer points for some time, then decided that Adam wouldn't be worried about apple pie as there was no cream in those days. Fay waited patiently until we'd settled our differences and Mack's nose had stopped bleeding, never mind the handful of hair missing from my ginger head.

She read on. "And Cain lived seventy years, and begat Mahalaleel..."

My curiosity was aroused. "What does begat mean, Fay?"

"Begat? Well, it means..."

I saw with surprise that she was going red in the face. "We will leave the Bible lesson now and I'll read a chapter from *Gulliver's Travels*..."

"*Robinson Crusoe* is better," Mack suggested, but younger brother didn't agree.

"I want *Gulliver's Travels*."

"So what? I want *Robinson Crusoe*."

"*Gulliver's Travels!*"

"*Robinson Crusoe!*"

They were at it again. Not that I minded. Watching them kick and punch was better fun than trying to do lessons in all that midsummer heat. Mosquitos coming in the windows and all.

· · · · ·

Suddenly, Father was standing in the doorway, wearing his most pained look. "Fighting, and your sister with the Bible in her hands, reading to you? Don't you know the children of God do not fight?"

Mack regarded him sulkily. "Want to bet?" he asked.

The Brocas family at dinner. Harold in World War I uniform at the rear, beside his fiancée; Mother standing beside Father, at the head of the table; Nora at this end, second from the left.

III

Accident-prone

I was always a great admirer of my brothers' horsemanship, probably because I was too scared to learn to ride. To me my brothers were daring heroes. They seemed to deliberately court danger and take it almost as an insult if their horses refused to buck, bite, or try in some more subtle manner to unseat their riders and if possible break their necks.

Father, in what I can only think of as an absent-minded moment, bought the boys a copy of *Bar-20*, Clarence E. Mulford's Wild West novel. There must surely have been a sale of Western rough-and-tough novels in the Hokianga at the time. Hopalong Cassidy's influence was felt strongly all over the district. The Hokianga became almost overnight one great wide-spreading rodeo.

My brothers were the toughest riders of them all. Even when still at primary school the dangerous delights of buck-jumping had begun to pall. They looked around for fresh fields to conquer and came up with the idea that it might be fun to try to ride Father's beef bullocks running wild out the back of the farm.

These were mad-headed beasts, uncontrollable and highly dangerous. Not like Father's working bullocks which were trained to accept wooden yokes and were accustomed to drawing great loads of logs behind them. Father would have had something to say if the boys had tried to ride on the backs of these useful and friendly animals of his. I don't doubt he'd have had something even more forcible to say if he'd known about the wild bullock project, too. He may at times have found his large brood of youngsters a bit of a headache, but he certainly wouldn't have wished a broken neck onto any of us.

The boys finally managed to run one of the huge bullocks into a rope trap — a snare was I think the correct term — and from the overhanging branches of a tree lowered the most daring of their buck-riders onto the beast's heaving, incredibly arched back. With the wild-eyed animal fairly cornered the other boys obligingly passed a rope under its tummy and tied the rider's feet together. Nothing could dislodge him now, short of the rope breaking.

Great satisfaction was expressed by all humans present, though I must except myself. I took no part in the proceedings and had forfeited the right to even comment — I was up a tree some distance away, terrified and bawling loudly as usual.

The riding arrangements really went very well indeed. It was only after several successful buckjumping rounds of the paddock that the bullock found the perfect comeback. It decided to roll on its rider. The result, several cracked ribs and Heaven only knows what other injuries. The poor lad must have been in agony but no one told the grown-ups how he got hurt. After all, Hopalong Cassidy would have made little of such minor injuries.

The boys went back to riding horses as against the more exciting bullocks, but even horses had their playful moments. Edgar was bucked off and injured his back rather badly, then just to show they were not to be left out of the fun, the huge Clydesdale draught mares Father bought from the defunct Auckland Tramway Board took their turn at the game of Beggar-My-Neighbour.

Father was kicked on the knee and put out of action for some time. It was meant to be a playful kick but those huge hooves carried all the impact of a pat from an elephant's foot. I felt sure the Clydesdale would have been quite upset if it had known the trouble its playfulness caused. Father was in hospital for a month or so anxiously watching a large patch of skin trying to graft itself neatly over his injured knee. When he came home, he sold the horse to a neighbour who was looking for a broad-backed mount to transport a young family of six to school.

Six youngsters on one horse's back must have looked like a camel gone haywire but amazingly the horse didn't mind. Those kids treated that huge creature as one of the family. They even piled in under its wide tummy to keep out of the rain and it never raised a foot to dislodge them.

But even if the horses really meant to act reasonably, one nip of a fierce brown-and-yellow horse fly would send them round the bend.

It would be just my luck to be in the saddle when this happened. If it were a horned saddle with the popular Mexican-style wide wooden stirrups, the rider might well have an urgent appointment with death.

We had on the farm an elderly retired racehorse Father had bought for a song. He came to us bearing the unusual name Schneider, goodness knows how he came by it. He was nondescript, neither brown nor bay in colour, with large innocent childlike brown eyes.

A friendly horse, he'd poke his head over the fence to greet anyone who had time to stand and talk. Butter wouldn't melt in his drooling old mouth. He really was quite old and going grey in a strawberry-blonde sort of way.

Mother once rode him out to the back of the farm. Father wanted her to glimpse the beauty of a grove of kowhai trees in bloom near the far boundary of the five-hundred acre farm. So he dug out an old side-saddle and persuaded Mother to take this ride out over stony scoria land, with him walking at the horse's head all the way. Schneider behaved like a lamb.

Shortly after this I caught my brothers making preparations to visit an old apple orchard at the back of the farm. I hated the boys to go anywhere without me, but in that blistering Northland heat I hesitated to follow along behind their horses on foot all the way over the red-hot scoria dust.

They kindly offered to take me up behind the saddle, but I was, perhaps unfairly, a bit cynical about this arrangement. I knew I would certainly die of terror if they started their horses bucking even ever so playfully.

"Try riding Schneider," they suggested. My probing glance caught no hint of sniggering smiles on their faces. Perhaps I really could trust the old horse to treat me gently? After all, Mother had been safe enough on his broad and woolly back.

So on board Schneider's obligingly immobile old back I was duly hoisted, and we set out in convoy for our destination. This was rather fun. I began to wonder why I had never found the courage to do this sort of thing before. Fancy being scared of old Schneider!

But now the scoria land was behind us, the smooth heavily-grassed river flats rolling out beneath our horses' trotting hooves. No rocks on which a nitwit of eight years could bash her ginger head if she and the horse parted company rather suddenly.

"Want me to teach Schneider to amble?" the question was put enthusiastically to me. "All good horses amble. You know, something like a broken cantering motion. DER-rum-ter-rum-ter-rum-tum-tum. White horses prancing in Wirth's circus, remember?"

It sounded attractive and would certainly be easier than the way I was being jogged about like a sack of potatoes when Schneider broke into a trot. I thought yes, I'd give ambling a go.

"What you have to do is to hold the horse's head in with a tight rein and belt him with your riding switch. It won't hurt him, he's got a hide like a rhinoceros."

They were paying me flattering attention, the three of them. I guess being the centre of interest must have gone to my head. All right, if they wanted me to make Schneider amble that's exactly what I would do. With any luck I'd come out of this not looking such a cowardly idiot.

They were all three watching me, the reins slack on the necks of their own horses. This was my big moment. I held the reins tight and switched my trusty steed in the ribs.

The next thing I remember is coming slowly back to consciousness. I was lying on the ground. Blood had had time to dry around my mouth and nose. My tongue felt as though it had been put through a mincing machine, my head pounded and I felt desperately sick. I could see two or three of everything within my sight. I remember wishing the ground would keep still instead of rocking like a crazy hammock.

Schneider was nowhere to be seen but I vaguely realised I still held his bridle in my clenched fist. I must have pulled it off over his head as I took a somersault.

One of the boys was saying in a scared tone, "We didn't know he'd buck so hard. He usually just pig-roots."

Another of my fond brothers was feverishly trying to force between my lips a handful of squashed ripe blackberries. He was deadly pale, his expression suggesting that he fully expected me to die of malnutrition before I could recover my scattered wits.

Some time later I made one last trembling attempt to master the gentle art of horse-riding. They say a horse knows when its rider is nervous. Be that as it may, my mount began at once to pig-root and act the fool, putting its foot through the stirrup where my own foot by rights should have been. My brothers watched proceedings with hilarity. "He sure knows how to use a stirrup. If he's getting into the saddle you'd better get off." It was an old gag but fitted the occasion. I slid to the ground and that was that, I'd remain a live coward rather than a dead heroine. After all, there must be thousands of people in the world who can't look an honest horse in the face.

Shortly after the Schneider incident I stepped into the path of yet another accident coming my way. One of my elder sisters was ill with a nasty bout of influenza and it was clearly my duty to cheer her up. I offered to sing some Moody & Sankey hymns to her but she shook her head quite decisively.

I was surprised and disappointed. I had intended to sing, "Keep me unspotted from sin, dear Saviour," a great favourite of Granny's. This hymn tied in with my sister's own childhood. The family had had a dear old cow called Spotty, and for years my sister thought the words they sang almost every Sunday night were, "Keep me and Spotty from sin, dear Saviour." She must have wondered how come the other cows on the farm were not restricted.

Still, singing was obviously out. Perhaps I could show the invalid how to plait a round whip, using four strands of flax? I'd just learnt the art and was proud of myself. But not that, either. "Run outside and play, chicken. I'm all right by myself."

But I wouldn't dream of deserting her. Gymnastics might prove cheering, she could then try one of the acts herself when the flu left her. I did two long-legged headstands on the end of her bed, then turned a somersault — crashed onto the floor and did something quite unfunny to my neck. I carried my head at an odd angle for months afterwards.

The family came to know that a wild yell from me didn't necessarily spell elation or youthful exuberance, it merely meant that I had unguardedly tried to turn my head. Father's anxiety made him seem sharper than he meant to be. He'd shout at me, "Get your head up straight, you silly girl! Are you going to walk like a wet duck in a thunderstorm for the rest of your life?" I had been wondering the same thing myself.

• • • • •

Mother brought up the question of a visit from the Rawene doctor but the suggestion was received coolly. Father pointed out it was hardly worth paying seventeen pounds sterling to have the medical man come and tell me to straighten my neck. He'd told me that a hundred times already and if I refused to obey him it wasn't likely that I'd take any notice of a similar order from the doctor.

It sounded a logical enough argument. After all, £17 is a lot to pay out on an accident-prone liability. A red-headed snivelling young coward, hardly as yet worth the salt she ate. I was even scared of the cows we helped to milk and had been known to drop a bucketful of creamy milk on the cowshed floor if a cow so much as twitched the tip of its bushy tail.

So I put up with a dislocated neck and even became accustomed to the discomfort, but when violent toothache added to my miseries it was just too much. We youngsters pulled out our own teeth if they were loose enough, but this was a double tooth. I knew it was well rooted because I'd heard the dentist say during one of our rare visits, "What a set of tusks this one's got! Look at this, Nurse. Her mother must have been an elephant!"

I was left to wonder how such an unlikely thing as an elephant got into the conversation. Still, I picked up the general idea as the dentist sweated and grunted, pulling out a back tooth. His own teeth weren't so hot either, but that was understandable. It must be awfully awkward for the only dentist in the district to have to pull out his own teeth. "Open wider, please. Now you can swallow if you wish to. Wash your mouth out with this pretty pink water." He'd feel such a fool sitting in front of a mirror giving himself the inevitable dentist-chair advice.

He'd feel a fool, too, if he knew he'd missed a decayed tooth in my mouth. I found out about it when I was one of a gaggle of youngsters being towed round and round the ploughed paddock on Father's clod-crusher, our combined weight being destined to roll out the cultivated ground as smooth as a city lawn.

Six of us were on the flat wooden crusher enjoying our bumpy ride when suddenly the ground seemed to come up and hit me and at the same moment the sky fell on my head. I let out one unholy yell. The frightened horses did two rounds of the large paddock before Father got them under control again. Even then they were trembling and sweating and inclined to take off again at any second.

"If you think this is a joke…" Father's moustache bristled angrily. I said hastily I didn't mean it as a joke, I had the toothache. That was what made me yell. And of course I began bawling.

"Well, get off the sledge, then," Father suggested. "We can't have you howling and yelling like a Red Indian behind the horses. The animals are quite upset."

I was quite upset also but I didn't think it was a good idea to point that out just now. I wouldn't get any credit for having merely yelled out when terror struck me whereas the horses responded to their panic by completely losing their heads. Now if I had gone galloping madly in all directions with the sledge bobbing and bouncing along behind…

Oh, well. Never mind. I tumbled off the sledge, shaking the dust from the folds of my print frock. A young lad staying with us for the holidays said hopefully that he had the toothache too, but it didn't work.

"You stay where you are," Father ordered sharply. Fair enough, I suppose, even though the boy was bored to death, sitting on that dusty thing all morning. He certainly was a fattish lad and sat nice and heavy on the clod-crusher.

My skinny legs were taking me at the double towards the house when Father called after me, "Don't go worrying your mother, d'you hear? She's not well today."

Thrown abruptly onto my own resources, I thought of the painkiller the grown-ups used for toothache but I wasn't keen about using it. Somehow the cure was more unendurable than the toothache when that vitriolic lotion took over. I could think of nothing I could do to put an end to the agony. The worst of it was I couldn't even ask God to help me. After all, He must have known the decayed tooth was there in my mouth all the time, so why didn't He draw the dentist's attention to it? Even if He was very busy it wouldn't have taken a moment of His time to jog the dentist's elbow, sort of.

"What's wrong with you?" My elder brother appeared on the scene. "Don't say you're bawling about that crooked neck again? I wouldn't worry, kidlet. Anyway, you look quite unusually intelligent with your head on one side like that. Don't forget the ducks are the cleverest creatures on the farm and they're always cocking their heads sideways and staring up at the sky with one eye…"

"Oh, pipe down!" I bawled ungratefully, "I've got t-toothache, bad. It's awful."

He seemed deeply touched. With all the confidence of a trained dental surgeon he said, "Come on up to Father's workshop and I'll yank the tooth out for you. No trouble."

I can't remember whether I told him the tooth wasn't loose. Probably I didn't mention that all-important fact.

"Sit down there with your back against the anvil." He had a big pair of not-too-clean pliers in his hand. "And don't yell, it isn't going to hurt much. I'll get that tooth out in a jiffy, you'll see." His manner was quite professional.

He got a good strong grip on the double tooth near the back of my mouth. I think it was two rounds of the large workshop we made together, me on the business end of the pliers, my brother white-faced and sweating but determined to finish the job.

I was too scared to yell. If anyone came out of the house to see what was going on we'd both get into trouble. At the point where I knew for certain my jaw was broken, the tooth came ripping agonisingly out, leaving a great jagged hole. And at that stage my elder sister came through the workshop door.

She was angrily threatening to sit him on the impromptu dentist's chair and pull out every tooth in his head, if it took her all night to do it, when her voice began to fade in my ears. I went out cold in a faint.

Amazingly, the gum healed quite well in spite of the rust and dirt on the pliers. I got away with fobbing off the adults by telling them my face was swollen with toothache and I couldn't open my mouth. Only too true, I couldn't open my mouth.

I remember my brother gave me a shilling and promised to feed the calves and hens for me for a fortnight, which he did. So everyone was happy.

It was some days before I awoke to the fact that my head was perched straight on the top of my neck for the first time in months. Something must have slipped into place while I was being towed

· · · · ·

round the workshop at the end of the pliers.

I said to myself, "You see? Our family Friend hadn't let me down after all, He'd meant me to be dragged around at the end of the pliers so as to get my neck straight. He must have meant it to happen that way when He forbore to point out the bad tooth to the dentist." My heart was warm with gratitude.

Our parents encouraged us to stand around the piano singing Moody & Sankey hymns. My mouth was too sore to let me sing, but with one finger I picked out a tune on the piano. "God moves in a mysterious way, his wonders to perform." I felt that whoever wrote that hymn certainly knew what he was talking about.

I recently discovered in Father's old diary an entry which seems to tie in with my accident-prone existence. He'd written, "I'm very much afraid we are to be blessed with another addition to the family." That blessed little accident was me.

IV

Ententertainment a go-go

Life in the Hokianga was not all hard work and noses to the grindstone. Dances, for instance, were popular with all age groups. Father put down a terrific dance floor when our large front room was built. We held dances there fortnightly, tidal rivers and other unpredictable circumstances permitting.

People would come long distances, by launch, rowing-boat, canoe or on horseback. Everyone brought contributions to the supper. If a basket dance was announced the single young ladies were expected to supply a special supper packed into an attractive container or small basket. This was offered for auction at supper time, going to the highest bidder, who not only bought himself a delicious supper but also gained the privilege of enjoying the supper dance with the pretty young donor.

There was much winking and nodding when a basket was offered, competition becoming very sharp and keen if the donor was known to be a good cook. If she was not a good cook but could claim to be the prettiest girl in the room, competition among the male bidders was just as eager. Proceeds from the auction went to the Red Cross or some such worthy cause.

Blank dismay registered upon the faces of young bloods who accidentally bought the wrong basket and found themselves paired off with a girl in whom they were completely uninterested. Much bargaining went on behind the scenes before everyone was sorted out to the general satisfaction.

In some ways this was a cruel custom. A girl's popularity could be seen by the rush for her basket, yes, but on the other hand the measure of her unpopularity was gauged by the lack of response in the bidding. I can imagine some heartburnings among the young men, too, when they found themselves out-bid and had to see their choice swept into the supper dance in the arms of a rival.

We youngsters had great fun preparing the floor for these dances. First we'd shred candle grease over the floor, then we'd skate madly in all directions on old sacks or discarded woollen garments until the surface was like glass. The final treatment was a sprinkling of boracic powder. Everything was ready for a GoGo evening. Death and damnation to anyone who walked across the floor in wet or muddy shoes! Get the floor damp and the evening would be ruined for the dancers.

Traditionally the evening began with a slow waltz. Then there might be a Charleston or a two-step. By this time dancers would be warming up and could be excused for really letting themselves go in a rousing Schottische, with a hoot and a stamp at every turn.

Some of the livelier sparks, not all young either, would engage in a Highland Fling which would almost rattle Mother's best vases off their wall brackets, to say nothing of the glass wall lamps shifting precariously on their perches.

Square dances were popular; Quadrilles, Lancers, d'Alberts. And out in the bedrooms half a dozen infants would sleep through it all, or if they didn't sleep no one would hear their wailing protests. Not above all that din.

Alcohol was unheard of at dances but soft drinks were served copiously throughout the evening. No one smoked. About two in the morning thoughts would turn unwillingly to the early muster of cows. Milking normally began not later than four thirty; if the men were lucky and didn't live too far away they could be home by then.

There was of course always the question of river levels. Not much sense in shedding white cotton gloves and dark jackets ready to drive the launches home if there wasn't enough water in the river to float a rowing boat, even. A few gambling spirits might make a dash to catch the last of the out-going tide, but as often as not they were stranded high and dry on the mud for hours. To plead that the launch got stuck on the mudbank was equivalent to protesting that the car had run out of petrol.

Actually, nothing can be more uncomfortable than spending the night in a wretched old tub of a launch stuck on the mud and keeling over at an angle of umpteen degrees. Impossible to cling to the cabin seats, so everyone sprawls on the launch floor, ranged decorously like sardines neatly packed into a tin. You're lucky if someone has remembered to bring a warm rug. Early morning fogs can be deadly cold on the banks of a tidal river. Tempers fray as mosquitos move in.

The newly built school down-river was more central than our home, so eventually the dancing venue was moved there. There was no piano, but dance music was provided by local players of the accordion, the more complicated piano accordion, violins and 'cello. Very satisfactory and inspiring music.

After years of holding the festivities in our own house, we now had to get out our launch and proceed down the river, but we didn't mind. If anything the launch trip added to the fun. Often we didn't reach home in time to go to bed at all. Father would be already up and dressed, so there was nothing else we could do but strip off our good clothes, climb into denims and turn out to milk the two hundred cows.

Any child who had not mastered the gentle art of milking cows by seven years of age was looked on with scorn in the district. Likewise it was considered absolutely stupid for any young farmer to court a girl who was useless about the farm and milking sheds. There was no bonus for a pretty face. If a girl fell in love with one of the local farmers she'd know better than to admit she'd never milked a cow. If she were keen enough she'd set to work secretly to learn how it was done. Such is the power of romance! Learning to milk a cow is not as easy as it looks.

But back to the festivities. Once, to please Father, Mother went along to one of the dances at the school. Born and brought up in the English cathedral town of Shrewsbury, Mother never quite grew accustomed to swift flowing, muddy rivers with their rickety landing wharves. Especially at night.

However, we all reached the school without incident. The dance floor was comfortably filled and everyone in a gay mood. High spirits were probably due to the fact that the dairy factory had closed down for the winter months. No more turning out to milk the cows in the mud and the rain, not until the factory reopened next Spring.

Supper was a marvellous exhibition of what some home cooks could do with half a dozen pounds of the best Jersey butter plus a gallon or two of cream and unlimited big brown eggs. The whole tone of the evening was perfect.

Someone spilt a cup of coffee over the babies sleeping in the corner of the room but the coffee wasn't hot enough to wake them. No one worried about the incident apart from a few hurried exchanges of ideas for coffee stains, the removal of.

Home time seemed to come round all too quickly. We packed up, filed down the hill and were standing on the wharf waiting for our turn to scramble into the launch and take off up-river when suddenly, loud and clear above the chattering and laughter, there was the sound of groaning, creaking timbers. Before anyone had time to wonder what was happening, much less time to retreat, the wharf collapsed, spilling its human load into the greasy, porridgy slime of the riverbank twenty feet below.

Lanterns went out. People screamed blue murder, calling the names of relatives. Panic took over completely. Impossible to imagine how everyone emerged none the worse from that ghastly mud bath. If the tide had been at its highest there would have been drownings there in the pitch dark.

We arrived home as the dawn was turning the blue line of the Waima ranges a lovely pale pink. My younger brother leapt out helpfully onto a log beside the wharf ready to fasten the mooring rope, but sprang back into the launch just as quickly.

"What d'you think you're doing?" Father barked.

Young brother came right back at him, "I know what I'm not doing! That isn't a log I was standing on, it's a very drowned horse." The flood waters must have carried it there. If I remember, he actually burned the shoes he had been wearing when he stepped onto the 'log.'

We filed sleepily onto the porch, and almost fell over a small crate which certainly was not there when we left for the dance. The neighbouring Maoris had been round and left us a little silky-black wild pig from the forest. Their kind thought seemed to round off a memorable evening.

Later our entertainment was to become madly sophisticated, taking in the first travelling circus to visit the tiny village of Taheke. Glamour had come sunbursting into our lives. To us there was

• • • • •

nothing shoddy or sordid in the grimy red and white striped tents and caravans, and though the animals did look thin and tired, we didn't doubt that they would be given a good meal before they were bedded down for the night. Still, it wouldn't have taken long to have combed out the mangy old lion's tangled mane.

Then there was the travelling 'talkie' that came to Rawene. Father almost had a stroke when he found he had to pay out four shillings a ticket at the hall door but he later agreed that was the best four bob's worth of entertainment we'd ever had.

The talkie picture was not meant to be funny, it was a rough'n'tough Western. Tragedy stalked the rancher's daughter, and only those men whose trigger finger was always at the ready lived to tell the tale. We were expected as an audience to be shedding buckets of tears, but it didn't work out that way.

The talkie machine was a mobile one, the first of its kind, and something had gone wrong with its timing. The action trailed seconds behind the voices. The hero would be saying, "Kiss me, you beautiful thing, you! I have waited all my life for this moment," and at the same time delivering a mighty punch to the villain's chin.

"I'll teach you never to do this to me again, you sneaking, two-timing cur!" and the lovely heroine would be at that precise moment clasped in a close and passionate embrace, lips locking in slow motion.

The travelling company offered to refund the money for the tickets if the patrons were proposing to utter a complaint against them. No one was. We all voted it top-line entertainment. Young gallants of the village re-enacted the touching scenes for weeks, their timing just as absurd.

Another social highlight: (this notice was stuck to corrugated iron).

❦

The district dairy factory picnic was the highlight of our year. Everyone wandered happily about in the tropical heat of the northern summer eating ice creams especially made for the picnickers. Watermelon was the big feature of the day. For threepence one could buy a huge crescent moon slice of juicy pink and white melon, more than you could possibly eat. You weren't with-it if your face wasn't submerged in luscious melon most of the day.

Inside the factory everything was polished to the nth degree. Fascinating to watch great sheets of rich cream pour down over the coolers before being channelled into churns so big a man might well stand upright in them.

Someone thoughtlessly slammed the door of one of these huge mechanical churns. There was a man inside, one of the factory staff presumably washing it out. Through the glass panelled door we caught a glimpse of his terrified face peering out. It wouldn't have been funny if the churns had started turning.

I remember being shocked, even scandalised, to meet up with one of our visiting parsons at the picnic. Ministers of the church were not meant to enjoy themselves! He was actually hogging a great welter of pink ice cream! And only the Sunday before he'd, literally, put the fear of Hell into us kids, shouting and Bible punching and warning us where we might expect to end up if we dared to sample the fleshpots of the wicked world.

If rare and exotic ice cream wasn't one of the fleshpots I would, in that moment of disillusionment, very much like to have been told what was. My soul shuddered at the thought that he might have given way to other temptations such as gutsing luscious melon. It wasn't fair to threaten us with Hell and damnation then turn around and eat from the fleshpots himself.

V

Grist to our mill

Good Christians should always show brotherly love toward their fellow men, Father impressed upon us. Fair enough, but the mill hands in Father's timber mill slipped up a bit on showing brotherly love towards us children. Good Christians or not, they hated the lot of us. Our young lives were clouded by mysterious threats. "If I ever catch those blasted kids..." or, "Hanging's too good for that bunch of young cut-throats."

And all we ever did to bring down their wrath upon us was dig traps in the sawdust. We'd dig a deep hole, cover this with a 'lid' of thin interwoven strips of wood, so thin they would hardly take the weight of a dog. Scatter sawdust over this lid and all we needed then to complete this charmingly light-hearted project was the unsuspecting passer-by.

Our wide-eyed innocence when we just happened to be around to see a mill hand disappear up to his waist must have been the hardest part of all for the victim to bear. I wonder no one had the good sense to murder the crowd of us.

There can be no more exciting playground than a five acre, twenty feet deep mountain of warm, clean sawdust. The canyons between towering ramparts of sawn timber offered great scope for hide-and-seek but we always returned with pleasurable anticipation to our sawdust arena. On our more successful days we could expect to catch five or six mill hands in our carefully concealed booby traps.

It must have been more by good luck than good management we never trapped Father. I'm sure he wouldn't have taken the men's complaints so lightly if he himself had ever had the earth drop away from beneath his feet. There was a definite risk of broken limbs but we didn't realise that at the time. We were merely a bunch of innocent kids making their own endearing fun. (I think I hear the mill men's voices chorus, "Oh, yeah?")

The best fun of all was digging tunnels into the heart of the sawdust mountain. This was excitingly dangerous. We had been strictly forbidden to tunnel even a few feet into sawdust but the temptation was too great. Besides, we didn't realise just how lethal the operation might be. The warm damp sawdust packed together with deceptive firmness and if the roof ever did look like sagging we'd prop it up with boards borrowed from the mill. After the first few feet the going became tougher, mainly because we lacked the means to light up our field of subterranean activity.

All this came to a sudden end the day the tunnel roof collapsed. My youngest brother and I were the only civil engineers on duty that morning. It was a Sunday and I think we felt guilty right from the start. Still, we managed to stifle our consciences and went to work with a will, sawdust flying out the entrance to the tunnel in fine style. A busy beaver had nothing on us two when it came to burrowing.

I had backed out to find a more effective bit of board to dig with. When I turned to report back for duty there was no tunnel. The whole thing had caved in.

I stood and stared. Where was Edgar, anyway? Unless that slight hump away over there was him? I couldn't be sure. When I stamped on the hump there was no response from beneath my feet.

I took off for the house as fast as my skinny legs would carry me. They were sitting down to a Sunday dinner of roast sirloin of beef, roast kumaras, Yorkshire pudding, peas and potatoes. On the sideboard reposed a huge fruit trifle decorated with crystallised cherries, whipped cream, and some green strips called angelica, I think. All this registered even through my panic. I forgave them for their gluttony — after all, they didn't yet know Edgar was buried alive in the tunnel.

No one seemed to notice me as I approached the long dining table so I blurted, "Edgar's in the tunnel."

There was no reaction. Grown-ups don't always listen, and anyway they probably wouldn't know all that much about tunneling. If I'd said Edgar was in the river they'd have gone tumbling over each other to fish him out.

I tried rather timidly to attract Father's attention but the buzz of talk and the settling into chairs went on. "Edgar's in the tunnel, Father," I tried again, but still he didn't hear.

"Tell-tale," Brother Mack withered me with his scorn. Tale bearing was frowned upon severely, partly because it tended to undermine one's own feeling of security.

I poked out a resentful tongue at him. "Mean little sneak," he retorted. We all knew tunneling was something one didn't discuss in the hearing of grown-ups.

"I'm not telling tales…" I'd begun to cry. "I only said…"

"Stop your quarrelling, you two," Father barked, "Don't let me have to take the strap to you."

If I wished to save my own skin I'd have to be a bit more explicit, and fast. So, blubbering and snivelling, I gave them the works. "Edgar's buried himself in the tunnel and he can't come out. He… he didn't answer when I stamped on him."

That should bring some action. At least they were listening this time. The whole family took off, even Granny. I got myself out of the path of the human cyclone, scooted out the back door and made a beeline for the slight mound which I was fairly certain was my dear brother.

He was hauled out none the worse for the experience, he'd had the presence of mind to curl himself up like a hedgehog when the sawdust began to collapse. Quick thinking for a six-year-old.

"You see?" Father's moustache bristled accusingly. "If you hadn't been so disobedient this wouldn't have happened."

He was probably right but I couldn't help feeling quite sure God kicked the sawdust into the tunnel because He wanted to teach us a lesson for playing so frivolously on a Sunday. If we'd been standing around the piano singing Moody & Sankey hymns He wouldn't have brought the roof crashing down to half kill Edgar.

Next Sunday I'd take out insurance for the whole family by sitting like an angel on the couch reading *Shine Your Little Light* all day. Not that I was displeased with God. If He felt it was His duty to tumble the sawdust in on top of Edgar, who was I to argue the point with Him? I was pretty sure He didn't like punishing children, anyway.

Like when Granny smacked us. "It hurts me more than it hurts you." That was a curly one, but we had to accept that an old lady with grey hair and take-out teeth wouldn't say it if it wasn't true.

Father started a flax mill operating, or reopened the mill. I think it was on the farm when Father bought it. We children were terrified of the whole flax-milling complex, perhaps because of the long lines of ghostly looking bleached tow swaying mysteriously in the breeze. Nor was the huge wooden scutching wheel mercilessly flaying tons of green flax an inspiring sight.

After the wheel deliberately scutched my favourite cat we decided among ourselves the wretched thing was an instrument of the devil. There would probably be dozens of that type of flaying wheel in Hell, a place in which we were morbidly interested. We never even considered the possibility that we might be admitted to Heaven. Our shortcomings weighed heavily upon us.

All the same, we were startled when real crime brushed us. Someone was trying to get away with Father's logs up in the bush. Every log had been branded with Father's personal insignia, his initials interwoven, so how the thieves imagined they could overcome this difficulty goodness only knows.

We were soon to learn the details of their plan. With a cross-cut saw they crept into the bush under cover of darkness and sliced off the branded ends of the logs. All that remained to be done was jack the logs downhill into the river and float the raft away out of Father's sight.

Father had his loyal Maori friends to thank for scotching this well planned trick. It would be a mighty smart Pakeha who could succeed in putting one over our Maori neighbours. Their watchfulness saved Father a considerable sum of money; he wouldn't have had a hope of proving a claim for unbranded logs once they had been launched into the river and floated away.

Timber rafts on the Hokianga rivers were always a fascinating sight. Half a mile in length, the huge logs bound together by means of iron dogs — wedges with an eye for the threading of wire rope.

Father was never a raftsman himself. He couldn't swim a stroke and shared my distaste for drowning. In any case there were Maori raftsmen eager to take the job. The rafts these men put together were really something. A truly professional work of art. The whole performance would have made a fascinating TV presentation.

• • • • •

The element of danger was never absent. Men had been known to slip through between the logs and drown, but the threat didn't worry our raftsmen. They ran about constantly on the moving raft, helping the tow launch to keep the logs clear of the riverbanks. If by ill chance a log should break away, some young Maori would volunteer to ride it back to the raft, sitting astride if it were small enough or squatting on the log and guiding it with his furious paddling.

Logs sawn ready to be floated to the mill sometimes washed off the riverbank and went careering sideways, lengthways, even end over end towards the sea. Daring young men rode these logs, also. They did it for fun, or because they had no canoe handy in which to travel downstream. In any case, only an idiot would risk his canoe in those raging flood waters.

The rider had to keep a careful watch for other logs taking a vicious poke at the one he was riding. The booming crash of two runaway logs colliding could be heard for a great distance. A foot or a leg caught in that murderous charge… well!

My brothers used to concede it took guts to ride a log down river in a flood. It also took skill and great daring. The nearest we children ever got to doing it was a brief run across logs when they were safely moored at the mill wharf.

Logs held a fascination for us country kids. We felt almost sorry for them, hounded as they were by launches and raftsmen, roped together and mobbed into tight, tidy, subdued armies. Sliced eventually into neat, mathematical lengths for use by builders. What an end for such magnificent giants of the forest!

But there was one type of log no one had any sympathy for. A mean, nasty, sneaking log with a vicious, treacherous personality. A 'sinker' was bad enough, Heaven knows, and an ever-present menace to launches, but at least a sinker fell to the bottom of the river and stayed there so that it was possible at low tide to chart its whereabouts.

The launchman's worst enemy was a 'bobber.' An apt description. These strange logs, always large, dive down out of sight then come shuddering up till almost half their length is towering above the water. Then down they go again. They give the appearance of restless

Logs ready for milling.
NORTHWOOD BROTHERS PHOTO CIRCA 1910.
ALEXANDER TURNBULL LIBRARY

whales coming up for air every dozen yards or so. There is nothing to be seen on the stretch of water ahead of the launch, when suddenly this huge, mad creature attacks from below. As for the fate of a rowing boat — oh, brother!

No one seems to know why huge logs behave in this ridiculous and undignified manner. Launchmen could swear the creatures are endowed with a lethal playfulness. Some say that mere buoyancy brings the bobbers up again, but surely buoyancy to that degree would keep the logs floating all the time, as all normal logs are expected to do. And if there were no buoyancy at all they would sink and stay down permanently. Also, why should the majority of bobbers be white pine?

Crossing the Cashel Street bridge in Christchurch recently I looked down at the lazy, charming Avon river and I thought — gosh, don't you ever go mad, crashing great logs together with a thunderous boom and drowning people! The Mallard ducks looked up at me and seemed to laugh loudly at the mere suggestion.

I can't picture timber scows from Sydney making their way up the Avon. When the scows came up the Waima river to load timber at Father's mill, their width filled the river from bank to bank. The displacement of water was spectacular. Any craft unfortunate enough to be on the river had to get out of the way, but plenty of warning was given by the scow's siren hooting almost non-stop. And of course the progress of so large a sea-going craft had to be very slow along the confined waterways of the Hokianga.

The scows moored at the mill wharf for three or four days while timber was loaded. This was an interesting interlude for us children. We were strictly forbidden to go near the scows at any time, but every evening we would sit at open windows and enjoy the rousing music which beat its way across to our eager ears. We wished the crew would never put away their accordions and mouth organs, their tin whistles, violins, 'cellos and kettle drums. Most of their singing was in languages we couldn't understand but was no less musical for that.

When a scow left it had to back down river to the nearest creek, half a mile from the mill. With much shouting of orders, ringing of bells and wielding of long pike poles, the stern of the ship would be manoeuvred into the creek. Obligingly the ebb tide would catch the bow and swing it downstream. In an amazingly short time the scow would be on its way, headed back to the harbour bar and out to sea.

We children felt terribly important and wished our city acquaintances could see us standing on the riverbank being farewelled by ear splitting blasts from the ship's siren. The crews never failed to wave farewells as long as we were in sight.

I think many of the members of the crew were reminded of their own children at home in Sydney. They could also be wondering if they would make the journey back across the Tasman Sea in safety, if they would reach their homes. Even at the start of the return journey there was a real hazard to be faced, the unpredictable gateway to the Hokianga Harbour.

Sailing ships were claimed by the Hokianga harbour bar in the early days of northern settlement. In 1929 the cargo ship *Isabella du Fresne* was flung upside down and sank there with the loss of all lives, and she was not weighed down almost to the Plimsoll line with timber as were the scows from Sydney.

We heard of a terrible quarrel the crew of a visiting scow had, all over a bottle of whisky. A full bottle was accidentally dropped overboard into deep water at the mill wharf. One of the crew volunteered to dive for it, but when he regained the ship with the bottle in his hand the quarrel began. The other men accused him of opening the bottle underwater and taking a great swig of whisky. We children argued for days as to whether this would or would not be possible.

Living near the mill was an old Maori chief, wrinkled and generously tattooed. He was an honourable old man whom everyone respected, Pakeha and Maori alike. He used to take a great interest in the shipping that went on at the mill. It seemed to us he looked with contempt upon the Pakehas' clumsy ships. Not like the long, slim, graceful waka of his younger days.

Those waka proudly displayed their hand-carved figureheads as they slipped with almost effortless grace through the waters at a faster pace than any plump, lazy old timber scow. But then the timber scows did not have fifty or more bronzed warriors driving them through the water with inspired paddles.

Logs being transported by water at the Hokianga branch of the Union Box & Packing Case Co at the Rawene Mill.
NORTHWOOD BROTHERS PHOTO CIRCA 1910. ALEXANDER TURNBULL LIBRARY.

And ready to ship.

VI

Manna in the desert

I was sitting on a large scoria rock on the back yard drying my ginger mane when the family cat, also a bright ginger, went rushing by, hissing and growling and glaring at me with insulting suspicion.

"Stop that cat!" my sister-in-law yelled, "It's got a thrush in its mouth!"

"Too late." I didn't even bother to climb down out of my rock seat. "The thrush is dead."

"I know that, silly!" Sister-in-law came pelting up the path. "It's the thrush I want! The cat hasn't begun to eat it…"

"It's dead," I repeated stupidly. For heaven's sake, what could she want with a dead thrush? And why rob the poor cat?

"I'm going to make soup out of it. Aha — got it! Sorry, puss."

The penny dropped. We'd been without meat for more than a week. No eggs. The hens had stopped laying for the winter months. Even our vegetables were in poor supply.

Usually we lived rather well, cream every morning on our porridge, plus all the butter we wanted on our crisp home-made bread. When we felt we'd appreciate a change of diet it was our custom to get out the rowing boat and take off down the river catching mullet.

No hook or line or fishing net was needed for this sortie, we merely rowed the boat close in beside the reeds along the riverbank. The startled mullet did the rest. Leaving their feeding they'd leap high in fright, to fall back into the boat.

Our normal catch on a good night when there was no moon and the tides right was around forty to fifty fish. Some we would give away, some we smoked in our tin smoke house. Fifty large mullet took some using up, and there were plenty more in the river when we needed them.

But since the river was at this time in high flood, fishing was out of the question. Even the eels had dug themselves in along the muddy banks. We were in sorry straits indeed, though we wouldn't actually sink to starvation point. There was plenty of flour in the house. Tea and sugar also. But what a boring diet!

After a brief but bitter struggle, Ginger Cat had scooted off, growling deep in his throat. Minus one plump thrush. At the corner he paused to look back at sister-in-law, hating her. It was obvious he would never trust a human again and would make sure no one ever set eyes upon his kill in future. Who knows when they might fancy a nice fat young rat, snatching it away from him?

Mother was an excellent provider but there were times like this when providing for a large household must have seemed a Herculean task. Granny's contribution to the situation was not exactly helpful, either. She had a habit of reminding Father there were plenty of beef cattle on the farm if he would only bestir himself and go and kill one of them. She knew Father could never bring himself to kill any of his animals.

Did Granny go to market over this 'weakness' of his! But if it weren't the food question she'd have found something else to quarrel with Father over. Mother must often have wondered how come two such devout Christians should love each other so little.

Not that Granny appeared to work hard at her religion. Normally she hardly seemed to bother God at all with her troubles, she was more inclined to lay her complaints at Father's door. But there were times of stress when she would come out with a heartfelt prayer, "God, must I endure these young heathens forever?" The generation gap, I supposed.

"Either you go out and kill something or I do," she threatened Father, fire in her eye. "There's that sheep…"

"No! You can't kill my pet lamb!" I glared at her in horror. "Betty's one of the family, you might just as well eat Father!"

She muttered something under her breath which perhaps fortunately none of us picked up. "All right, then. That fat young porker…"

"That's mine!" Edgar shrieked. "If you eat Porky Pig you'll go to gaol for being a cannibal!"

· · · · ·

"Oh God!" Granny groaned. "Some of you take your guns and go shoot a pheasant if that's all you can manage. Or perhaps you'll tell me the pheasants are not rising in the rain?"

That was exactly what Father had been about to say, but she had cunningly cut the ground from beneath his feet. With a deep sigh he said, "Every man is given a burden to bear, it is meant to try his faith."

Granny came back at him smartly, "A man who fathers nine children has little time for practising his faith anyway."

The meaning was beyond me but the actual tone of the words sounded like the proverbs we had to take from our copybooks at school in writing lessons. I was fairly sure I could use this new saying at school on Monday.

In the meantime we sat down to yet another meal of hot scones and bread-and-butter pudding. There would be a riot if we couldn't get through to Rawene soon and pick up a good feed of tender juicy beef. Roll on summer with cold meats and salads... and blackberry pie! We drooled nostalgically.

Blackberry pies in the Hokianga are truly unique. I've never seen such large, luscious berries anywhere else in New Zealand. Blackberry pie with cream and brown sugar — oh boy! And half the enjoyment was in the gathering of the berries. Every season we'd picnic with other settlers at the old mission station, Lower Waima. Everyone went home with buckets full of the ripe fruit.

On these blackberry picking safaris we children would look longingly towards old Mrs Puru's fig trees growing among head-high gorse and blackberry vines. There was a barbed wire fence separating us from the trees, but we could see the fallen fruit lying thick and rotting beneath the trees. Beautiful figs as large as pears, purple-pink in their luscious ripeness.

The fruit was wasting, mountains of it, but our miserable consciences forbade us to touch even a mouthful of it. Not that there was much chance of taking the fruit anyway, Mrs Puru's dog saw to that. Legend stated that her Alsatian had torn off a man's arms and legs. There were even worse tales about the huge baying creature, blood-curdling tales every word of which we believed. The dog was said to have swallowed a thieving child whole in one gulp. Even this was easy to accept when listening to that deep threatening canine voice echoing back from the hillside.

Temptation moved in sharply upon us youngsters one hot February afternoon. The dog was in full sight from the blackberry patch below, tied to the verandah post of Mrs Puru's lonely little hut. The old lady herself was nowhere in sight.

We conferred hastily together and decided she must have gone visiting at the pa or Maori village across the Waima creek. If we were ever to taste those figs, now was the time. It certainly seemed safe enough to make a dash for the groves of trees, keeping low behind the gorse thickets just in case we should be spotted by the wolfhound. Not that it could possibly snap that solid looking chain, anyway. We were comfortably sure of that.

The manoeuvre proved highly successful. We stuffed our greedy little tummies with those delicious figs, staying to eat one more and yet another while we knew we should be getting out of there.

Suddenly one of the boys hissed, "She's coming!" They, my brothers, took off over the barbed wire fence with me streaking along behind them. I wasn't doing too badly and could have made the grade if I'd climbed the fence as did the boys, but I was scared of the vicious barbs. I chose to wriggle through underneath.

My blue cotton dress slithered up as I squirmed, and there I was, caught on the barbed wire by the seat of my strong blue bloomers. The thought swept briefly through my mind — the dog would most likely eat my legs first, seeing they were so handily suspended there under the wires right in front of his face.

Then he'd finish his grisly meal by devouring my arms, since I was at eight-and-a-half years old too tall to be swallowed in one canine gulp. It was merciful of God to have given me such long indigestible legs.

The terrifying rustling in the manuka scrub behind me grew louder, grew nearer. It could only be the old lady herself, if it were the Alsatian it would surely have had at least one leg by now. Unless Mrs Puru was holding the dog back until it planned its mode of attack?

Struggling and fighting to free myself, I was petrified by a great burst of laughter, the high cackling laughter of the aged. Witch-like

· · · · ·

laughter, I thought in my terror. Still laughing, Mrs Puru said something, but since she couldn't speak a word of English and I had only a sketchy grasp of her language I was none the wiser.

I couldn't see the Alsatian but that didn't mean it wasn't sneaking up on me from behind. I began my customary terrified bawling, continuing to kick and struggle mightily but my almost new bloomers would not rip.

Then unbelievingly I was being released. I think she said in her own tongue, "Keep still," but she managed to unhook me from the barbs anyway in spite of my lack of co-operation. Her high laughter followed me as I streaked off in the direction my brothers had taken. We piled into our boat and rowed down that creek as though the devil himself were after us.

We said nothing at home and since Mother had not noticed my torn bloomers we didn't have to think up any excuses. But next morning there was a sequel to delinquency. We found on our porch at home a huge flax kit filled to overflowing with gorgeous ripe figs. Mrs Puru must have prevailed upon some relative of hers to bring the figs to us, she was much too tiny and too old to have carried them all that way herself.

Mother and Father were much impressed by the old lady's generosity. They would have been even more impressed had they known the full story. It was a pity they had to miss such a unique opportunity to extol the virtues of turning the other cheek.

We children retired to talk over the situation and decided that, even if the Alsatian had caught me when I was trapped under the fence, Mrs Puru would in her generosity have allowed the creature to devour only one of my legs, leaving the other for my own use. No one could reasonably ask more than this of either her or her dog.

Next Christmas I received a beautifully worked flax basket, something I had always wanted. The woven colours were lovely. There was no means of telling where it had come from, but I knew old Mrs Puru was particularly clever at colouring and weaving the flax strands.

VII

Things that go bump

The night my brothers saw a ghost they were all in their bunkhouse tossing in the tropical heat of a northern summer and cursing the mosquitos swarming into the room. The door was wide open; only an idiot would try to sleep in a closed room during the summer months.

As the boys tell it, there was a huge orange moon just beginning to peep over the hedge some little distance from the door. Slowly, something white and shapeless and somehow... opalescent came drifting across the surface of the moon.

The boys didn't even pretend they were not terrified. "Give's my gun," one whispered, and was ridiculed for the suggestion. "You can't shoot a ghost, you nitwit."

"What're we supposed to do, then? In the movies ghosts don't go away when they're told to, they only clank and rattle and laugh not very nicely."

"Ask God to take it away," someone else suggested hopefully. "He could call the ghost back, especially if it's ... it's... what d'you call it..."

"Absent without leave? Don't be stupid! You can't say that to God!"

"Why not?" The prospect of a rousing argument was taking some of the bite out of their terror.

"Well... how do you know the ghost is AWOL? You're going to look a fool if it's been given permission to wander around..."

"There it goes again! It's getting closer..." Their first encounter with the supernatural was not funny. "Perhaps they're mad at us because I went to the fancy dress party dressed up as a ghost?"

"Huh! That was three years ago. You don't think they've been sitting up there for three years waiting to scare you to death?"

It wasn't a reassuring word to introduce at that moment. But at least the shadowy white form had gone.

"It hasn't, you know." The more daring of the boys slid his feet to the oil-clothed floor, crept soundlessly across the room and found his gun. After some fumbling in the dark he announced, "That's got it loaded. Now we'll see whether or not we can take a shot at a ghost."

"You can't do that! Suppose it's one of our own ancestors?"

"Oh, shut up and keep your heads down! For all you know a bullet could ricochet off a ghost and hit one of you…" By now the sharpshooting young tough was sidling courageously towards the outer door. He was halted by a wild yell.

"Cut it out, you lunatic! Don't shoot — that's old Donkey!!"

The decrepit old white horse was never to know how near she came to joining the equine ghosts that night.

"Are you going to tell Father?"

"What do you think? You know Father believes in ghosts. What's he going to say if we tell him we nearly shot one?"

They were quite right, Father did believe in ghosts. His interest in spiritualism began when he learned that Sir Arthur Conan Doyle was a spiritualist. Father had always been a fan of Conan Doyle's because of the interest the famous author had shown in the Brocas family history. Father's titled ancestors were mentioned in more than one of Sir Arthur's historical novels.

As a devout Anglican family we were all quite shocked by Father's defection. I think Mother was disillusioned also, for she made no objection when I rather defiantly made up my mind to go ahead and be confirmed into the Anglican church despite Father's lack of support.

I duly went forward for confirmation and almost had my neck broken as punishment for my disregard of parental mandates. In honour of the Archbishop's visit to the small country church the good ladies of the parish had worked like beavers varnishing every one of the long pews. When we young girls stood up to go forward for His Grace's blessing our veils had stuck to the new varnish on the back of the seats. Our heads jerked backwards in a vertebrae-dislocating jolt which would have seemed extremely funny on a less serious occasion.

And just to put me even further in the wrong, one of Father's ghosts made its presence known to me. I suddenly became a believer. It couldn't have happened in a more spooky place.

To draw water from our large rainwater tanks we had to navigate a long, narrow, dark passageway, an alley between the house and an outdoor lumber room. Being such a natural-born coward I always scuttled along this terrifying canyon and back as fast as the kettle-filling process would allow.

This evening one of our thirteen cats had chosen to sleep down there. In the dark I stepped on its tail. The shriek of anguish it came out with took seven years off the end of my life. As though this were not mortification enough, I was grabbed almost at the same moment by a practical joking ghost. No sensible ghost would have tried to scare the life out of me when it must have known I had in my hands a heavy iron kettle.

It could only be a ghost. Every one of the humans was in the living room playing five hundred. That's why the kettle filling fell to my lot. I was a lousy card player.

To this day I remember the ice-cold terror I felt when those ghostly fingers closed round my arm. I was too terrified to scream but I still had strength to swing the iron kettle, water slopping everywhere as I struck.

There was an agonised groan which bore no resemblance to any known human tones. I'd heard ghosts scream like that on the movies. Not stopping to feel around in the pitch dark for the kettle I took to my heels.

In the living room they greeted me with surprise. "Where is Mack?"

A silly question to fire at me. I didn't know where young Mack was, nor did I care. They were all staring. Even the old ginger cat on the calfskin rug by the fire sat up and waited, watching me with suspicious green eyes.

"Mack went after you," they told me. "He was supposed to carry the kettle back. It's too heavy for a skinny thing like you."

We'd failed poor Father again. He would have been so delighted had I been caught in a throttling grip by a real genuine ghost. As for myself, every last vestige of credulity had been shaken out of me by an old white horse, a sleepy cat, and a practical joking young brother.

There was no such thing as a ghost. One thing I did know, if I were ever proved wrong, if I ever did really see a ghost I'd die of fright right there on the spot and that would make two of us.

Still, we have no right to scoff at anyone's beliefs. Father might well have been right, and who knows? His belief in the supernatural is shared by many level-headed and clever people. Who am I to argue with them?

If we had told our Maori friends and neighbours ghosts do not exist they would have written us off as ignorant Pakehas. Their ghosts live on with them unseen but forever beloved.

Now I'm going to stick my neck out and record what happened to me not long after Mother died. I was reading in bed by candlelight and must have dozed off to sleep. The candle tipped forward and was setting alight the white woollen blanket on my bed when someone called my name, not loudly but so urgently I awoke with a start, only just in time to avert a catastrophe.

The voice was my mother's. Quite unmistakably. In any case, no one else could have called out, they were all sleeping peacefully in their beds unaware that I was about to burn the house down about their ears.

It seemed reasonable to accept that Mother's gentle, selfless love had not died with her physical withdrawal from our presence.

VIII

Farm for sale

"Yes," said the newcomer, stretching out his hands to the blaze from our mid-winter log fire, "I like the look of your farm. I'll take another walk round tomorrow and if everything continues to come up to my expectations I'll buy."

This was good news. Father was delighted but cautious. There had as yet been no mention of terms for the sale. If the stranger expected to get his hands on five hundred acres of good dairying land for an old song he had another thought coming to him. Father's moustache bristled aggressively as he expressed this opinion to his favourite audience, Mother.

No wonder he was being careful, he'd sold the farm once before and fallen in badly. The buyer went bankrupt, which meant Father had to come back trailing half a dozen of us youngsters and begin all over again.

Still, this chap gave a reassuring impression of strength and farming capabilities. He said he had been travelling throughout the Hokianga district in search of good land up for sale and he'd heard in the Taheke pub about Father's farm. Now he'd seen the land he'd decided it was the best in New Zealand. His manner of saying this was highly flattering to Father and to the quality of the land. We all thought he was terrific.

"Take your time to come to a final decision," Father said, barely managing to hide his elation. The deal now seemed certain. The scene was one of great cordiality.

After about a week of tramping up and down dale, of sampling Mother's excellent dinners and enjoying the comfort of our best guest room at night, our visitor casually announced his intentions. He'd take over the farm immediately. "I'll pull down that cow yard and build a bigger one, putting in concrete flooring and all modern facilities for the comfort of the cows and the milkers."

We all agreed he had a fine way of handling the King's English. He might even have been at some time a school teacher, before his obvious love of the land took over.

"The river flat I shall probably put down in wheat. There's good rich ground there, wheat should do nicely beside the river."

Like blazes it would. I could see the denial in my brothers' faces. They were imagining a waving crop of golden wheat slowly disappearing beneath the swirling waters of a flooded river.

Father did have the grace to say dubiously, "We-ell, I wouldn't promise there'd be no rust on your wheat. These river flats are wonderful growing value but they do get a little damp at times in the winter."

A little damp?? Oh, brother! Anything would get a little damp with thirty feet of river water on its head. My brothers would like to have pointed this out but were quelled by a blazing glance from Father's English blue eyes. Absolute frankness and honesty were not, it seemed, always the best policy.

"Yes, I'll put the flat ground down in wheat," the buyer nodded, well satisfied. "Now, about the higher ground, you'd run ten cows to the acre most of the year round?"

"Ten cows to the acre?" Young Mack's eyes stood out on sticks. "Come off it, Mister! Five cows…"

In a deadly calm voice Father broke in, "When I need your help or advice I shall ask for it, son." He was undoubtedly thinking if he had his life to lead over again young Mack would not figure in the family scene. "Get along out of here and don't come back, you children."

"Now, now," the guest put in a word for us, "you mustn't be harsh with such delightful kiddies. Let them stay, they really were not upsetting me. Now — what were you about to say regarding the five cows per acre, my boy?"

"Nothing," Mack said, mumbling. It was not the guest's disapproval he was worried about. Anyway, we stayed underfoot, clustering adoringly about this man who found our company so delightful. It was a word which sounded refreshingly different in our ears.

Father's elation finally began to show through. They'd agreed to go together to the Bank in Rawene next Monday to arrange details of a financial nature. They were suddenly old friends, real buddies, now the deal was irrevocably settled.

We youngsters began planning what we would take with us to the city. This was easy until we came to the list of pets. Our pet hen, ten years old and still laying big brown eggs regularly? A squawking old hag of a creature minus half the feathers and all the sense she was born with, but we loved her and she loved us. We couldn't find it in our hearts to abandon her.

There was of course the problem of trying to keep her in any sort of a hen-run. She'd managed to escape from even a maximum security enclosure. We wondered fleetingly if it would be possible to capture one determined old fowl from amidst the wheels of city traffic. No doubt the city police would be willing to take a hand.

We finally settled for two horses, three cattle dogs, one hen, my pet lamb and the old bull who so obligingly allowed us to sit on his broad black back when he was resting in the paddocks. Things were moving ahead to our great satisfaction. We might well be in Auckland for the August school holidays.

Plans for the future buzzed about everyone's ears. Father phoned Rawene about packing cases, the local auctioneer was consulted regarding a sale of any cattle the new man did not wish to take over, our places were booked on the coach and train to Auckland. Of all that happy company our guest was the most joyful. He beamed upon all our arrangements.

He was not married, he said, but all the same we undertook to show him how the family washing was coped with. We took him to the sheds where Father had installed the steam boiler salvaged from the disbanded saw mill. There we gave him a demonstration of fire-lighting in the gigantic fire-box, of how to control the rising head of steam by opening a valve and yet contriving to keep out of the way when the steam shot its powerful jet roofwards.

Finally we came to the purpose of our lecture tour. Along the wall Father had installed large wooden tubs. It was our job to hand-pump water from the well outside, fill these tubs and immerse the customary mountain of household linen and clothing.

Right. Now to connect with a tap on the boiler a long rubber hose. Someone held the business end of the hose well down under water in the tubs, someone else turned the tap on, and hey presto! In an incredibly short space of time the contents of the tubs were leaping and frothing in gallons of boiling water.

Instant washing machine, but without the modern machines' safety margin. We made certain the steam pipe didn't escape our grasp and go twisting and turning and writhing in the direction of our guest. That powerful jet of steam would scald the flesh off his legs, in which case he might well change his mind about taking over the farm.

"What happens if the hose escapes you?"

We should have expected this question from so smart a man but it took us unawares. "You could get yourself killed…" Mack began. His voice trailed away. We could see him remembering the consequences of his unthinking bursts of honesty. *"When I need your advice I'll ask for it, son."* Father's tone had been far from cordial.

Mack swallowed, took a deep breath and said, "The hose never does go wild and even if it did you wouldn't have anything to worry about. Just hop across the floor and turn off the steam tap at the boiler."

Sure. If you don't mind having to avoid the lethal steam pipe by progressing across the floor in great leaps and bounds, ballet-like movements. The devil took over the writhing hose and aimed it at the nearest human. I knew this for a fact, as I was once guilty of letting it loose. The force of the steam tore the hose from my hands and it was that same force which refused to allow the hose to lie still on the floor for one split second.

Still, it got the clothes beautifully white and also served as a means of scalding the milking shed utensils, the cream separator etc. No doubt the danger added some spice to our young lives, but unfortunately the newcomer didn't look at it that way. He made it clear to Father that he would not under any circumstances consider using the devil machine, which decision would not have affected Father in the least if it had not been followed by a flat refusal to pay for the expensive equipment.

"You'll have to have the steam boiler torn down before I set foot on the place," the new buyer pronounced. "According to what the children had to say…"

Oh, dear. We all found urgent business as far away as we could get. After this episode relations between Father and the buyer became noticeably less friendly but we were not unduly concerned. After all, the deal had gone through, the buyer couldn't back out now. We decided to pour oil on troubled waters by taking the buyer under our wings for the rest of the day. Our soothing company might well be just the touch he needed to restore his former good humour.

We walked him out to the back of the farm to take a look at our very own caves. Huge scoria rocks had formed caverns in the earth large enough to house a family down there. Native fuchsia trees and koromiko shrubs hid the entrance which was just big enough to admit one person at a time. It seemed a bit creepy, slithering down into the dark, musty depths below.

We were as disappointed as we were astonished when our guest refused to explore the caves. Thanks all the same, he said. Perhaps he'd try it out later when he was living on the farm. Nothing we could say would budge him from this extraordinary stand.

It seemed rather bad manners to leave him standing at the pithead, so to speak, while we slipped in to see if the candle we'd left down there weeks ago was still in its place, stuck to the rocks. True to my reputation as the coward of the family I gave in almost at once to blind panic. I was fairly certain I would have at least a fifty-fifty chance of being accepted into Heaven but I wasn't keen on making the transition right there, stuck in a mouldy old cavern of a cave. Besides, someone would have a devil of a job lugging my inanimate carcase up through that cave entrance.

The boys were chattering away happily somewhere in the vast echoing vault. There was the faintest scraping of some tiny creature's slithering progress across the rock ceiling above my head. My subterranean yell must have been really something as I shot up through that opening.

Blessed, blessed sunlight! But my troubles were far from over. A great slab of a bull stood guard only feet away beneath the manuka tree which housed our guest. Our wild-eyed, trembling guest.

He said, ridiculously, "S-see if you can call the creature off, won't you? He's out to g-get me…"

· · · · ·

Half submerged in the cave again I protested, "He won't come away just because I ask him to."

"Well, do something, child! Why won't he listen to you? He is your bull…"

"He isn't," I shook my tousled ginger head. "Our bull is quiet, he never roars and scatters the dust with his horns like this one is doing. I've never seen this bull in my life before."

He said again, desperately, "Do something, child! You should be used to cattle, even wild beasts like this one. Try to frighten him away, that's a good little girl."

He should be used to cattle himself after all his farming experience but I was too polite to say so. Instead I made him a pretty fair offer. "I could ask God to get rid of the bull?"

When he seemed too shocked to answer I was forced to reassure him hastily, "I don't mean to ask God to kill him! Just chase him away."

He said then a dreadful thing. It was my turn to be deeply shocked. If I hadn't already been more or less suspended in mid-air with only the vacuum, the emptiness of the cave beneath me, I would have sworn the ground slipped from under me. My world rocked. He'd said, and meant it, "Don't talk nonsense. I don't believe in God, anyway."

That settled it. He and I and God against the ranting, roaring bull might have been victorious, but if I had to go it alone with only God on my side — no. I slid back down to rejoin the boys in the cave.

They had lit the candle and were having a fabulous time gathering together fairy-like skeleton leaves which had fluttered down through the opening, century after century. It was a fascinating pastime. By the time we surfaced we had enough leaves to carpet the living room at home.

"Gosh," my brothers looked guilty, "we forgot about him. Wonder where he got off to?"

A swift glance told me the bull had disappeared too, so there was no need to say anything about it. "I guess he's gone home to dinner," I offered, and was grateful that the suggestion was accepted without argument or suspicion. I had enough on my mind puzzling over the retreat of that angry bull.

· · · · ·

Oh, well. Trust God to find some way of scaring the brute away, even though He was rescuing a man who didn't believe He existed.

It seemed to me our guest looked uneasily at me more than once during dinner. He seemed to be feeling a bit of a fool but he needn't have worried. It wasn't my business to tell the world he was stupid enough not to believe in God.

After dinner he took the long gum spear and went down to the river flat to prospect for the kauri gum we'd told him about. He'd only have to jab the spear down into the ground and he'd feel the chunks of clear golden gum gritting against it. We'd dug up large quantities of the gum and sold it in Auckland but there should be plenty left for him to get at when he took over the farm.

Unfortunately he decided to leave the gum digging operations and follow Father across to the paddock where the bullock team was lodged. Like most of Father's animals these bullocks, trained to yokes, were treated as pets and would come across the paddock to accept carrots from Father's hands.

"They'll eat out of my hand like a baby," Father boasted, speaking over his shoulder to the man behind him. "See? Quiet as sheep."

"Let me have a go." Our guest selected a handful of carrots and approached the animals. They took one good look at him and off they went, prancing across the paddock like a pair of over-animated rocking horses. The last we saw of them for days was their hooves neatly clearing an eight wire fence in the distance.

"You stupid fool!" Father never withheld compliments when he was worked up over anything. "Don't you know better than to offer the bullocks carrots with your hat on?"

We caught the buyer studying Father rather strangely during the remainder of the day. No doubt he was thinking, fair enough to take one's hat off to a lady when one meets her, but these bullocks were no ladies.

We kids happened to know the bullocks were for some obscure reason terrified of Father's old straw hat. He always threw it off before he approached them with the offer of carrots. It might have been fairer to our paternal ancestor if we had taken the trouble to explain this to our guest.

We were quite sorry the buyer was leaving us on Monday. He

had to return to Auckland to conclude the business arrangements he'd made with Father. However, he extended to all of us a cordial invitation to drop in at the farm any time we were around that way after he took over. Very kind of him, Father beamed.

Early Monday morning Father went into his room to wake him and help him on his way to the train. He wasn't there. He wasn't anywhere in the house.

We were puzzled and worried about him. A man couldn't just disappear into thin air — unless he'd had a loss of memory or something equally serious?

Later in the day while everyone was still upset and wondering what should be done about him the police phoned Father. They'd heard a rumour that we had a stranger staying with us. Could it possibly be the man they were looking for? An escaped prisoner from Mt Eden gaol? A soft-spoken fellow, a clever sort?

He was, the police said, considered dangerous. Had we seen anyone answering to this and that description?

We had. But we never saw him again.

We youngsters put our heads together, muttering. We were badly shaken. Honesty, it seemed, was not the best policy in the stranger's copybook. When he was at school he probably missed that page in his copybook and went on to the next which, we recalled, spelled out in impressive lettering, FAIR WORDS BUTTER NO PARSNIPS.

Yet that didn't seem quite appropriate, either. Fair words had gained for our visitor two or three weeks of excellent board and lodging absolutely free of charge.

I was left with a tormenting doubt on my mind. How could God punish someone who didn't even believe there was a Hell?

Oh, well. Perhaps God would say, "I have news for you, my lad…"

IX

Is there a doctor…?

"Do you think you'd better get the doctor?" Father queried anxiously, but Mother was beyond making any decisions. She was never one to make a fuss over her indifferent health, we hadn't even noticed she was ill. Everyone was horrified when she collapsed at the dinner table. If the sun itself had failed to put in its daily appearance Father would not have been more upset.

"I think I'm just a little tired," Mother protested from the couch to which Father had carried her, "I didn't sleep much last night."

One of my brothers muttered, "I'll say she didn't get much sleep. None of us did," his tone full of meaning.

The boys had all been against Father's move to install large mobs of pigs on the farm. They argued that pigs were the least attractive of animals and moreover they could not be contained in the paddocks set aside for their use.

"Nonsense," Father scoffed. Pigs, he said, were lovable creatures and if given due consideration were extremely hygiene conscious. He eyed with suspicion the boys' deadpan faces and must have known they were fighting ribald laughter.

If given due consideration? As far as he knew, elder brother contributed, more poker-faced than ever — as far as he knew, due consideration would be a waste of time and building materials. Granted pigs were clever creatures, but imagination boggled at the prospect of teaching a couple of hundred piglets to pull the chain.

Father was not amused. He showed his annoyance by rushing off and defiantly buying up the first hundred black Berkshires. Perhaps he should really have pig-fenced part of the farm before inviting the busy, grunting, rooting porkers to take over.

Life became a nightmare to all of us except the pigs. They were having a marvellous time methodically cultivating Mother's lovely flower garden from the roots upwards. The vegetable garden disappeared overnight. Father got out of bed in the morning to discover a veritable battlefield, bombshell holes and all, where he had expected his lettuce, cabbage and tomato plants to be flourishing.

"Weren't you going to order pig netting?" Mother suggested gently.

"It has been ordered." Father sounded unusually sharp with Mother. "I'd like to know," he said, "how I am supposed to pig-fence the farm when there's no pig netting nearer than Auckland? Am I expected to walk to and fro a hundred miles carrying rolls of netting on my back?"

"Oh well, I'm sure you're doing your best, dear," Mother soothed.

Perhaps so, but doing his best didn't prevent the wretched creatures from rooting their way in under the house. There they moved in on a bed-and-breakfast footing. They spent the entire night rooting, snorting, squabbling and squealing, to say nothing of scratching their itchy backs against the house foundations. The harsh rasp of pig bristles against timber has to be heard to be believed.

As a consequence, sleep was a forgotten luxury in our house. Very wearing. All the same, even we youngsters could see there was something more serious than lack of sleep worrying Mother. But call in the Doctor? We couldn't recall such a suggestion being made in our house ever before. It seemed like anarchy or at the least, sabotage.

We younger ones were evenly divided in our aversion to doctors and policemen, never having had anything to do with either. The general impression among us was that one came out about even in dealings with either of them. If you were very ill and the doctor shanghaied you into hospital you'd die anyway. Cynicism was not uncommon among us. Hadn't at least two ninety-year-old river people met a fatal end in the hospital? If they'd stayed in their own homes they might well have lived on for another forty years or so. In that case we might have been prepared to accept the adults' verdict of death through old age.

As for the police, their ambition was to hang everyone by the neck until they were dead. Probably about half a day's work on the part of the policemen in charge of proceedings. Our grim imaginings took us vividly right into the death chamber.

So we were fully armed against the doctor's visit. We would have urgent business at the other end of the farm. We'd be wasting our time hanging around in the hope of rescuing Mother, anyway.

After hurried consultation out of adult earshot we decided to take the small rowing boat and make our way up De Thierry creek, a waterway bordering one boundary of our farm. But we were outflanked by the advancing party. The doctor came flapping up the path from the wharf, his sandals splaying the loose scoria vigorously.

I was one of the lucky escapees. Not so my youngest brother. Finding himself trapped by the doctor's advance onto the verandah, young Edgar did the only logical thing, he dived in behind a big grandfather chair in the corner of the room.

It wasn't such a good idea after all. The doctor came and sat in the chair.

Edgar never did describe his mental state during the next thirty minutes but we could guess how he felt. Being country kids we were all painfully shy at that age. Edgar did say rather bitterly later, if our elder sisters hadn't been so stupid as to offer the doctor tea and sandwiches there would have been no crisis. He was a busy man and if left to his own devices would have gone striding off after his visit with Mother.

As it was he sat there practically on top of Edgar drinking black tea and arguing with Father about spiritualism, matching dogmatic assertion from Father with equally dogmatic repudiation.

The argument began to get out of hand. Our visitor brought it to a close. "You're out of your mind, man. Not another word about ghosties, d'you hear? Ay, you're mad, right enough. You'll be seeing spirits busy doing your ploughing for you, I shouldn't wonder."

He was on his way to the door but turned: "You've got a fine pair of young girls there. A bonnie pair. I'll have the both of them."

"You'll — *what??*" Father's eyes stood out on sticks. After all, this is supposed to be a democratic country and women have had the vote for years. "It's not me that's mad!" Father diagnosed, "What the blazes do you mean?"

"I'll have the pair of them," the doctor repeated brazenly, "the pair of them, d'you hear? They'll make a fine pair of nurses. Matron will be pleased."

· · · · ·

"Oh — nurses," Father said feebly, subsiding, "That's different. No, you can't have them. I need them in the cowshed."

"Oh, you do?" The doctor's blue eyes began to shoot angry sparks. "Ye'll be saying your cows are more important than my patients?"

"Now look here…" Father's tell-tale moustache had never bristled more fiercely. But he was fighting a losing battle.

"I'll see the girls at the hospital as soon as their mother can spare them." The doctor picked up his utility oilskin coat and went striding away. Dynamic, unassailable. Poor Father had met his match. He knew it, but wasn't going to give in without a struggle.

"The two of the girls, mind." The doctor turned in the doorway. "No funny tricks, d'you hear? Both of them together."

The legendary Dr Smith

"We'll see about that," Father retorted, glaring.

The doctor's nostrils flared. "Spiritualism! Look you here, I'll give you a couple of pounds in money for every wee ghostie that ever shows its face my way, I'll promise ye that."

Most of this Edgar relayed to us later, the gaps we were able to fill in for ourselves. A bit stupid of the doctor to suppose Father would ever let his shed hands go nursing. Still, if the girls themselves wanted to take on nursing… but this we did not know. No one seemed to have thought of consulting the girls themselves.

Some time later the phone rang. "Tell those girls the matron's expecting them here at the hospital the moment their mother is on her feet again. We'll have the younger one later when she's old enough." The doctor's voice certainly carried well.

Father took over the phone. "Now look here, I told you before…"

"I can't waste my time standing here talking to you, man," we could hear his voice right across the room, "Send the girls down on the butter factory launch in a couple of weeks. That should give their mother time to recover." The phone went dead.

"What is the world coming to?" Father stormed, "I'll phone that

· · · · ·

71

bombastic Scotsman back and tell him what I think of him..."

"Better not," Mother soothed. We kids had the impression she was smothering bright laughter. She said, "The doctor is right, you know. They would make good nurses." The spirit of prophecy upon her, Mother added, "I shouldn't be surprised to see one or both of them ward sisters at the hospital, given time."

And so it came to pass, as they had a habit of saying in the Bible.

His success in campaigning for hospital staff must have softened the doctor. Shortly after the girls left home to begin nursing, a large crate was delivered to Father by means of the butter factory launch which picked up our cans of cream every second day at the wharf.

Father was as pleased as any youngster would be with a mystery parcel. Opening it, he found a rare, hard to come by, young tamarillo tree all ready to plant. Also included were rose cuttings for Mother's garden. The doctor had remembered her admiration for the champion roses in the hospital grounds.

"One could almost like the man if he wasn't so obstinate in his religious beliefs," Father conceded.

Mother's warm brown eyes dared us to laugh. It would be a sorry day when she ceased to support Father in all he said. Her loyalty sometimes amazed us, there were times when she must have been dying to tell him off. Still, he was the only man in her life. She could barely remember her own father, a sub-editor of a London newspaper. He died when she was in her fourth year. I think he must have been as gentle, as cultured, as was our Mother.

When I was seven, I was forced into a closer acquaintance with the doctor. I must confess I had to be almost dragged by the hair of my head along the path which led to his surgery. Once there my customary mulishness took the form of refusing to have anyone, even Mother, accompany me into the inner sanctum.

I knew about confessions, my closest friend at the city school we briefly attended was a Roman Catholic. Whatever confession I had to make now was for medical ears alone. It never entered my head that Mother would have already outlined to the doctor the reason for my visit.

"How are you today?" The doctor was in his most genial mood. I said I was very well indeed, whereupon he laughed and said wasn't it a bit of a waste of time coming to see him, then?

"Mother made me come," I said defensively. If he didn't want me in his surgery then that made two of us. I would rather have been almost anywhere else in the world.

He picked up a mechanical jack-in-the-box, played around with it for a moment then absent-mindedly handed it to me.

"You might as well keep it," he said, "I'm a bit old for that sort of thing now."

Then he said, "I think I know what's bothering you, lassie. You feel badly about it, don't you? Of course you do, but you shouldn't worry your head. I can tell you this, you're not by any means the first to shoulder this crushing burden."

Crushing burden? Big words in the ears of a seven-year-old. I began to feel important, especially when he wrote something about my case in the large leather-bound book on his desk.

"No," he said, "you're not alone in this trouble of yours. Mary Queen of Scots knew all about this and so did Napoleon Bonaparte, when they were your age. Rabbie Burns too, for all we know to the contrary. Even Rabbie Burns was a little boy of seven years once, you know."

My sense of importance grew. "What about Granny?" I suggested, greatly daring. He considered this gravely, then shook his head. "I think we'll leave Granny out of this, shall we?"

No doubt he was right. Granny wouldn't like being put on the list. When a lady is old and grey it's easy for her to forget she was once seven years old and perhaps had to shoulder Crushing Burdens of her own.

It was time I got on with the confession. I muttered, "I know about asking God, but He must have been busy somewhere else. He didn't take any notice."

"Oh, Lord!" The doctor rolled his eyes and groaned. "You kids are chips off the old block. Still, as long as you don't begin seeing your father's ghosties. One in the family is more than enough."

I wasn't sure what he meant and in any case I had now got up sufficient nerve to carry on with my confession. To make it plain just how black was the case against me I blurted, "I'm seven years old and I still can't help biting my nails."

He wasn't even shocked. Still, I suppose if Mary Queen of Scots…

I wondered if anyone had thought to console her for her shortcomings with the gift of a jack-in-the-box. All the way home, chugging along in Father's launch against the ebbing tide, I played with the new toy. It was a gay clown with a spring inside him. He had to be thrust down into the square wooden box and the lid fastened. When the catch was slipped, up he sprang to his full height, his red lips curved in a delightful smile.

Taking everything into consideration, I was pleased with my visit to the doctor. Even if I absent-mindedly began chewing my nails again till they bled I would still feel that God had not entirely turned His back on me.

But when we reached home Granny brought me down smartly off my rosy cloud. She was not pleased with me. In the first place it was not in her book of rules to seek medical advice unless one's case was already hopeless anyway. To add to my sins I'd forgotten one of my most imperative daily duties, cleaning the glass chimneys of the five wall lamps.

No matter how carefully the wide kerosene wicks were trimmed, they still managed to cloud the chimneys. By the end of the evening a cleaning job awaited me, a jolly good rub with newspaper. Washing the chimneys was too risky, no matter how carefully the glass was dried, crack they went the moment we put a match to the wicks.

"Come on, child, hurry yourself along. Your father will be coming in expecting his evening meal to be on the table and the lamps cleaned and lit and all. It's well to be some lucky folk, I must say."

I wasn't sure whether the lucky 'some folk' was meant to be me light-heartedly gallivanting off to the doctor's without cleaning the smoky lamp glasses and coming back plus a fascinating toy, or whether Granny was hinting that Father had a nerve expecting his dinner to be on the table. I decided to hurry myself along anyway.

Four chimneys were cleaned and shining and piled into the big Morris chair by the window while I put a final touch to the fifth glass. I always put the glasses in the same chair because they didn't roll out of that chair onto the floor and smash like they used to do from less comfortable chairs.

The Morris was Father's favourite chair. He came in now and, with a weary sigh, sat down heavily.

Of those four glass chimneys there was hardly one portion left larger than a two shilling piece. Father was skinny but he was six foot three inches tall and weighed enough to smash any glass he chose to sit on.

I can't remember whether they actually sent for the doctor but I know the bedroom door was locked for ages afterwards. I guess Mother had a busy time picking out all that glass. If I had been just a little bit more unselfish I would have given Father my jack-in-the-box to comfort him.

"You see what happens when you neglect your duties to go globe-trotting round the countryside," Granny sheeted all the blame home to me. "If you'd stayed home and got those glasses cleaned before lunch your father wouldn't be obliged to eat his evening meal off the mantelpiece."

We weren't allowed to answer Granny back but I couldn't help thinking it wouldn't have made any difference. If I'd remembered to clean those glasses earlier it would only have been his lunch Father was eating off the mantelpiece instead of his evening meal.

I was hideously shocked at some later date to find the doctor once again darkening our doorstep. All very well for us to collect jack-in-the-boxes and what-have-you at his surgery. I was still grateful even though the spring had broken and Jack lay in his box lethargically gazing out at an unfeeling world. But when the doctor intruded into our home there must be something serious wrong with the invalid.

The grown-ups couldn't fool me. The doctor's presence could only mean one thing, Mother was about to die. Mother! We had supposed she would be there always, as much a part of our lives as the air we breathed. There wouldn't be anyone to take her place. Not anyone. Mother was first with us ahead of Granny and — perhaps — Father. With us she was running a close second to God Himself.

I'd cried when my favourite cat got itself scutched to death in the flax mill and I'd bawled and bellowed the roof off the house when I discovered it was my pet lamb they were serving up at the midday meal. We'd all cried a little when Dolly, the quiet old Clydesdale mare, slipped into a bog and was sucked down out of sight before our helpless eyes. Even Father had tears in his eyes then, though Granny held that against him and said he was less than a man to cry over a dead horse.

I couldn't help wondering if Granny would say he was less than a man to cry when Mother died. Well, I was not going to wait around for that heartbreaking scene. If I could think of some way to work it I was going to be up there to greet Mother when she came trailing clouds of glory through the pearly gates of Heaven.

Aspirins were always kept out of our reach so they must be dangerous pills. I climbed up on a chair plus two fat books and got the packet. It took me much longer to swallow the lot one tablet at a time, washing them down with draughts of cold water. The whole packetful.

By lunchtime nothing had happened. There was a loud roaring in my ears, but I didn't feel sick, darn it. With no more aspirin in the house it was, I fully realised, now or never. If I didn't watch out, Mother would beat me to the pearly gates after all, and that I could never take. There are no compensating factors in a young child's heartbreak. I was just a snivelling coward, opting out.

Father's unbearable anxiety over Mother's illness showed through in an impatience with the rest of his blatantly robust family. I felt he was being a little too harsh, especially in view of the fact that I was about to die. I couldn't even promise not to report his harshness to Headquarters when I got to Heaven. Angels don't tell tales, I was sure of that, but I was no angel — yet.

My ears roared for a couple of days. Granny diagnosed wax on the eardrums and threatened to tie red flannel round my head if I grew more irritatingly deaf. Her other remedy was to set me weeding Mother's flower garden in the tropical heat of a mid-summer's day. This, she said, would melt the wax off my ears if I really was deaf, and if I was only pretending not to hear a bit of hard work would cure that nonsense, too.

Anyway, it must have been a pleasant surprise for Mother to find her carnation borders neatly weeded when she was well enough to walk in the garden.

· · · · ·

*'Ambulance' transport to the first hospital at Rawene.
Matron Jones is waiting to receive the patient.*
A.K. Woodley collection, Alexander Turnbull Library

Wharerakau, the second Brocas farmhouse on the Waima river — then and now.

X

Thanksgiving vacation

I'm sure Mother must have been both touched and delighted when Father announced his intention to take the whole family on a holiday to celebrate her return to good health.

"We'll take a week off," Father said, "and get right away from the farm. How does that appeal to you?"

"Wonderful," Mother smiled. We could already see the reflection of city lights in her brown eyes. Although she would never dream of saying so, we kids knew she sadly missed the city life to which she had been accustomed before she met and married a man with pioneering blood in his veins.

It was going to be quite a job transporting us all to Auckland, the nearest city. Quite an expense, too. Still, if this was Father's way of giving thanks, who were we to argue? We began to squabble over the question of transport. There were two choices, we could board Jimmy Cope's six-horse coach at Taheke and be spirited across the old gumlands to catch the train at the Kaikohe railhead, or we could go down river in Father's launch to Rawene and there crowd onto the coastal steamer, *Rimu*.

"We'll be going in the coach and train," someone guessed.

"I think it will be the *Rimu*," I said hopefully. I liked the *Rimu* very much. Even when it was such a rough sea we couldn't get into the harbour across the Hokianga bar I wasn't troubled by seasickness. Not so Father, he was sick before the ship even left the Rawene wharf. Which probably set the seal on travelling by sea, unfortunately.

Oh, well. The coach journey was fun, too, especially when the six horses were feeling their oats, as the saying goes, and trotted gaily along the dusty gumlands road, harness jingling excitedly. All the same, we were still feverishly anxious to know which way Father had decided upon. In the end we thrust young Edgar forward to ask the crucial question.

We were at lunch. Father put down his knife and fork and we saw with misgiving the familiar impatient bristling of his moustache. "Who said anything about going to Auckland?"

"You did," Edgar managed to blurt out, "You said we're going for a holiday."

"But not to Auckland," Father blandly kicked the props from under the lot of us, including Mother. She looked as startled as anyone. "I'm taking the launch up a side river," Father went on. "We'll camp in the launch and on the riverbank nearby. You elder girls will be in charge of the meals, and your brothers' job will be keeping us in firewood for the open fire."

"You said a holiday," someone gasped, and Father said sharply, "I said a holiday for your mother and that is exactly what this will be. Your mother won't have a thing to do from morning to night but sit and read, or perhaps enjoy herself fishing in the river."

"But... I don't like fishing," Mother protested faintly. "I'm sorry, dear, but you do know I can't bear to see the poor little things struggling for breath when they're lifted from the water."

"Fish don't breathe," Father spoke rather shortly. He said, "I hope you're not going to be unreasonable? I've been to a lot of trouble to arrange this holiday for you, my dear. Right in the middle of the busy dairying season, too. It hasn't been easy finding some responsible person to take over the milking sheds while we are away."

"That's a point," Mother brightened hopefully. "If you're worried about the farm I'd be quite willing to stay at home and keep an eye on things."

Father looked hurt. "You know I've always wanted to camp up the Mangamuka river gorge — and of course it will be a restful holiday for you, too. But if you really don't want to go..." he paused expectantly, knowing full well Mother wouldn't disappoint him.

With a stifled sigh she said, "Very well. I'm sure you will love playing in the forest there, children. There'll be lots of lovely trees to climb..."

"Oh no, there won't," Father said grimly, "This is a protected area, a national parkland. Just let me catch you youngsters climbing around in the trees — well, just let me catch you, that's all."

Mother took in our gloomy expressions and was spurred on to make one last ditch stand. "Granny won't be happy camping out. You know how she reacts to mosquito bites."

"Yes, I know," Father's tone was bright. "Your mother wouldn't enjoy herself. She'll be staying at home."

We all immediately developed an inordinate concern for Granny's well-being if she were left at home alone, but it didn't get us anywhere. It became painfully obvious we were all destined to keep the notorious Mangamuka mosquitos company on the banks of the river, the penal term being one long seven day week.

It seemed we were to camp just outside the forest reserve, pitching our tents in the corner of a friend's farm. Our tent, I should say. We girls were to sleep under canvas while the boys slung their sack hammocks in the farmer's trees nearby. Mother was allocated the comparative comfort of a mattress on the floor of the moored launch. Father brushed aside my offer to keep her company in case she was lonely or nervous in the launch alone. He said it was plainly his duty to give up the unique and pleasant opportunity to sleep in a hammock ashore. He'd keep Mother company.

When the appointed day arrived we edged our way up the tidal river more or less without incident though there was some excitement when the launch threatened to knock off her keel on a submerged rock in mid-stream. Father had to reverse the engine and get to work shoving the launch free with a long, vicious-looking pike pole.

The weather was perfect. Only one small snag marred our evening meal, there was not one skerrick of dry wood to be found anywhere along the riverbank. Plenty in the forest, of course, but it was against the law to touch that.

In the end we roasted the sausages one at a time over a small primus stove unearthed from a locker in the launch. It seemed an awfully long time before everyone was fed. Darkness was upon us to the tune of morepork calls from the surrounding trees and a melancholy booming of the bitterns along the bank.

At least, we hoped it was the bitterns. It wasn't altogether reassuring to reflect that the bitterns' strange deep note had often been known to merge quite deceptively with the enraged mumbling of an angry bull. The two sounds were quite indistinguishable even to the keenest ears.

"Of course it's the bitterns," Father said, preparing to retire to the nearby launch, "But you'd better have the pike pole ashore with you just in case."

"Can we have the lantern too?"

"What on earth would you want a lantern for?" Father's voice came irritably out of the darkness. He didn't even bother to answer when we said we wanted to play euchre.

Outside our tent the boys began initiating themselves into the gentle but highly acrobatic art of sleeping in a hammock. We listened appreciatively.

The mutterings and the bone-smashing thuds onto the hard-packed ground went on for some time. It's not so easy to stay in a hammock if you've never tried it before. Quarrelling broke out and that too went on for some time. Their voices were loud but we couldn't truthfully blame them for our wakefulness. As my sisters remarked, it wasn't so much the boys and the croaking frogs disturbing us, it was the zooming in of myriads of famished mosquitos.

We were suddenly aware that the squabbling outside had quietened. The ever-loving brothers had become united in a common danger.

Something was coming clumsily through the trees.

"Give me the pike pole, I'll shy it at the th-thing."

"No! You can't do that! Suppose you speared one of the farmer's cattle? Or his wife, or something? It would be murder..."

"What would the farmer's wife be doing prowling around the riverbank at ten o'clock at night?" Mack was always logical. He said, "Anyway, the farmer hasn't got a wife, he's a bachelor."

The crashing sounds came nearer. We girls were terrified but couldn't see any point in dashing to the rescue of the young warriors outside. After all, it was they who had the pike pole.

"Those bitterns weren't bitterns at all, they were wild bulls roaring," Edgar's voice came through to us, carrying conviction. So it would be wild bulls crashing towards our camp site.

"Now!" hissed one of the young men on whom our lives

depended. We didn't need to be told it was the signal to let fly with the iron-spiked pole.

There was an almighty roar from the darkness. The name of the Almighty was loudly mentioned, which struck me as being a bit unfair. It wasn't God who threw the spear at the farmer.

Fortunately the missile missed its mark but the whole incident seemed to be strangely repugnant to the irate man of the land. Even Father's hasty arrival on the scene failed to pacify our visitor.

It's a pity, he raved, glaring into Father's lantern-lit features, it's a great pity if a man can't walk along his own riverbank eel-trapping at night without half the damned brats in the Hokianga ganging up against him. And by the way, who gave Father permission to unload his brood of young murderers on decent harmless farming territory?

"You gave me permission," Father's temper was rising to match the newcomer's. It can't have been much fun for Father standing on the banks of a mosquito-infested river in the dead of night clad only in an ankle-length calico nightshirt. He brought his nightshirts from England with him and would not be persuaded even by family ridicule to give them up. At least he never had a nightcap to match.

"I never gave anyone permission to camp on my land," the farmer sputtered. "What do you take me for, a raving imbecile? And put that damned lantern out, Moses. You're bringing in the mosquitos off the bulrushes."

"Now look here…"

"You can stay till morning, but if you aren't on your way by eight o'clock I'll have something more to say to you."

"Who do you think you are, anyway?" Father flared. "And what right do you have to throw us off Tom Spence's farm? I tell you I have permission…"

"Tom Spence?" The stranger roared with laughter. " Man, have you made a fool of yourself! Tom Spence farms miles away from here in the Mangamuka Gorge, right alongside the national forest reserve. I take it that was where you were supposed to make landfall?"

Poor Father. Even the boys felt sorry for him. He faced us sheepishly in the morning light. "Well, that's our holiday. We're going home."

Our mosquito-bitten faces distorted in swollen grins. We couldn't have agreed more heartily with the verdict. Granny might be surprised by our early return, but then again she might not be. In her estimation everything we elected to do was a deliberate and carefully planned flying in the face of the Lord, so no doubt our humiliation would appeal to her as just punishment.

In actual fact we found Granny rather subdued. The local drill Sergeant Major had turned up there shortly before our arrival. His mood was not exactly angelic.

He stormed at Father, "Those two eldest boys of yours have missed compulsory military drill for two months running. What have you got to say about that?"

"Nothing," Father said blandly, reminding us sharply of his sons when they found themselves in a similar tight corner. He was in no way over-awed by the threatened brush with authority. "I told you I can't spare the boys from the farm at this time of year. I have nothing to add to that."

"You can't spare them from the farm?" The man in khaki uniform stared incredulously. "How come you can take a week's vacation from the farm then, the whole damn pack of you?"

"A week's vacation?" Father looked stunned. We hadn't known he was such a good actor. "Who told you that stupid story?"

"I did," said Granny, tight lipped. "A thanksgiving vacation, that's what you said with your own lips."

"Granny must think Father's a ventriloquist," Edgar muttered, "if he could talk through someone else's mouth."

The Sergeant Major rounded on him. "You need a bit of my army discipline, my boy — and by God, that's what you'll get when your time comes."

"I won't have any foul language around my family," Father's moustache had never bristled more aggressively, "If you can't keep a rein on that blasphemous tongue of yours..."

"Blasphemous? Oh, my God! Where did you grow up, in a Sunday School? You haven't heard anything yet, old timer. Why don't you come along to parade with your sons? We'd teach you a thing or two, I promise you."

"Teaching my boys bad language isn't enough, is that it?" They were both standing like hot-headed young cockerels squaring off for a death-or-nothing fight. "Turning up in your launch at the wharf whistling my boys off to parade like dogs coming to heel without their hats! You don't even give them time to finish the morning milking before you drag them away..."

"Like dogs without their hats!" The Sergeant Major gave way to chuckles which were in themselves an insult to Father's intelligence. But then the grin left his face as he snapped his heels together and turned to the boys. "You'd better be at the next parade — or else! Next Monday's the day, remember."

"Next Monday?" My elder brother eyed him with childlike innocence. "Next Monday's regatta day at Horeke. The Taheke pub will be closed."

The territorial cadets paraded at Taheke, as we all knew. The parade ground from which they were dispatched to points north, south, east and west of the compass was in fact the back yard of the hotel itself.

"You're sure the pub is to be closed?" He was eyeing Big Brother with suspicion. "In that case... well, I don't want to be too hard on you lads. Or on you, sir." The swift change in his manner was really something. "If you really do need the boys, Monday...?"

Father looked down benevolently into the other man's plump face. "Not at all," he said, suddenly the cultured English aristocrat. "I can spare them next Monday. I shall be at the regatta all day, myself. Since you've been kind enough to give me warning I'll see that both boys are ready and waiting on the wharf for you."

"With their hats," someone muttered daringly, but the drill Sergeant was no longer amused. He was caught in his own trap and well he knew it. To have to put in a whole day actually drilling the cadets... oh no! That damned pub...

"The lads would like to see the regatta themselves, I'm sure. I could get the parade cancelled, you know..."

"I wouldn't dream of asking you to do that. No, the boys will be ready for you next Monday. Won't you, boys?"

"Too right," they chorused. What was a stupid old launch regatta as compared with one long ecstatic day of playing now-you-see-us-now-you-don't, their victim a frustrated and thoroughly bamboozled drill master, their battleground several hundred acres of wild native forest. To say nothing of countless dips in the delightfully cool waters of the Taheke river.

"We'll be ready for you Monday next, sir," they promised brightly. From the expression on the Sergeant's face he didn't doubt their word for one moment.

Father was on top of the world again, fabulously pleased with himself. After all, he'd lost a terrible lot of face during the thanksgiving vacation incident. It was only fair of God to give him a good innings now.

The Sergeant made one last desperate effort. "Of course, if you feel your family needs a break away from the farm who am I to crack the whip over their shoulders? The weather's good, no sign of rain, and I could personally point you to one or two marvellous camping places. Down at the mouth of the harbour, for instance, or there's a beautiful spot up the Mangamuka Gorge river..."

"Thank you," Father spoke with deadly politeness, "but my plans are firmly settled. I shall go to the regatta and you will be given what you've been so... aggressively... demanding, a long, hot, tiring day on parade with your cadets."

"You're too kind," the drill Sergeant muttered venomously, and Father replied sweetly, "Don't mention it. It's a pleasure."

The sun was really shining for Father once again.

• • • • •

"Mother" — Rose Brocas, née Boughey: pioneer woman, patient wife, prolific mother, and poet of peace

XI
Shadow of the law

"Guy, want a word with you. What's this I hear about a bullock? They tell me you took your gun out the back of the farm and shot a bullock belonging to our neighbours. What have you got to say for yourself?"

Nothing, apparently. Guy just stood and stared mulishly back at Father. We others knew the story but it was not our place to butt in. This was a personal confrontation between the two of them.

Father said again, incredulously, "You took your gun and shot a bullock belonging to someone else?"

"I might have," Guy muttered, studying the toes of his boots.

"You *might have?!*" Father's attitude was one big italic exclamation. "Did you shoot the animal or didn't you?"

"I might have."

Father looked baffled but changed his tactics. "Now listen, son, I'm not going to punish you, I just want you to tell me, did you or did you not kill a bullock belonging to someone else?"

"I might have."

This was too much. Father stormed, "You'll give me an answer or you'll take the punishment of your lifetime. I've given you a good Christian upbringing and this is all the reward I get. A liar and a cattle thief. My own son! But you still have a chance. Now, tell me the truth. Did you or did you not deliberately take a stroll out to the back of my farm and just as deliberately shoot that poor animal?"

Guy looked at him. "I might have."

"All right," Father began to take off his wide leather belt, "you have the choice. Will you take a beating from me or shall I report this to the police?"

"Neither," Guy muttered, "I've never said I did shoot the bullock."

"But you did, didn't you?"

"I might have."

"Dear God, give me patience!" Father breathed. "Hold out your hand."

We stayed to see Guy get four of the best across the palm of his hand but by now were badly shaken and no longer sure we ought to keep our mouths shut. We might well have known we'd be dragged into the inquiry.

Ignoring the 'didn't hurt me' grin of defiance Guy was wearing, Father turned to me. I was just a second too slow in fading out of sight behind the boys. "What do you know about this disgraceful thing? Did you see your brother shoot this poor creature?"

Snivelling and as cowardly as ever I took a leaf out of Guy's book. "I might have," I muttered, kicking the loose scoria dust with my bare toes.

For a moment I feared I was going to be given a taste of the belt, too, but after a suitably aggrieved silence Father left me and advanced upon his next witness. "I know you'll tell me the truth, Edgar. Did you see this shocking massacre of an innocent animal?"

Edgar shuffled his feet, looked first to Guy for a lead, then to me. We both let him down, returning his glance blankly. He knew what to do. If he'd decided to turn tell-tale and dirty sneak that was his business, we were not the guardians of his conscience. All the same…

I kicked him on the ankle and was gratified to get immediate results. "I might have," he gave the delayed answer to Father's question.

Our paternal ancestor was showing signs of extreme exasperation. It began to look as though we were all going to get a touch of his belt, after all. But first he stormed at us, "Did you children see the bullock shot or did you not? And the first one to say 'I might have' goes to bed without any dinner."

As it happens we were all sent to our rooms without our evening meal. It must have been a gruelling afternoon for Father. Four youngsters becoming so utterly mulish he must surely have expected us to begin braying at the moon. Our doors were locked but the grown-ups never seemed to realise that we could communicate, room to room, by opening our big second floor windows and leaning out beyond the limits of safety.

"You going to tell?" Guy sat on the high window sill carelessly whittling a willow stick. I leaned further out from my vantage point twenty feet of blank wall away. "Of course not." The mere asking of the question was an insult.

The other two boys appeared on the sill beside him. "If you tell we'll burn your new doll."

I knew they wouldn't but they must have been desperate before they'd even mouth such a ghastly threat. I said, "What will happen to Guy if anyone tells?"

"Prison, of course. If he pleads guilty he could be in prison for the rest of his life."

"Don't be stupid, a life sentence is only for murder or manslaughter. For bullock slaughter he'd only get a few years."

We argued the point for some time, displaying a heartless disregard for Guy's finer feelings. We'd got as far as comparing his possible fate with that of the Man in the Iron Mask when he came into the conversation. "When I've finished with this willow stick whistle I might tell Father I shot the bullock."

"King's evidence," Mack nodded wisely. "You can get off with a caution if you turn King's evidence."

Guy snorted. "You can't turn King's evidence against yourself, you fathead. Besides, Father really means to send me to prison."

"Why tell tales on yourself, then? We'll keep quiet about seeing you shoot the bullock, honest we will."

"You didn't see me shoot it, you only heard the shot. You were all up a tree, too scared to go near the bullock. Anyway, you can tell if you like. If Father makes me go to prison he'll have to come with me. You'll see."

"But..." We were all gaping. Had his troubles turned Guy's brain? We'd heard Granny speak of one's sanity giving way under an unbearable strain, and she always seemed to sigh and look hard at us kids when she said it.

We assured Guy almost tearfully we wouldn't say one word if he'd promise to keep his own mouth shut and not give himself up to the law, but he was not making any promises. There was a strange glow of triumph about him, and this worried us even more than his seemingly irresponsible statements.

We were released from our rooms later but Guy's fate remained a mystery. We supposed a police visit was pending; Father had been on the phone more than once since our release. But instead of the police it was a neighbour who sought him out.

He said, "I've had a look at that dead bullock and it isn't one of mine. I've never set eyes on the ugly brute in all my life before."

"I've been waiting to hear from you," Father grumbled, "That animal should have been buried days ago. What took you so long in coming?"

"Well, you can bury it now," the neighbour said cheerfully, "If anyone comes kicking up a fuss and claiming that starved, mangy beast you'll be entitled to put the police onto him for cruelty to dumb animals. Good Lord, you can see for yourself the creature died of starvation!"

"It didn't," Guy butted in, "I shot it."

"Well good on you, son," the visitor beamed his heartfelt approval. "If I'd seen the poor brute lying there in that pitiful state I'd have shot it myself. It was suffering from two broken legs as well as all its other troubles. I never can bear to see animals in distress."

"Neither can I," Guy muttered, "That's why I shot it."

"You could have explained to me, son." Poor Father was obviously overcome by remorse. "Why didn't you tell me the truth about this?"

"I wasn't worried," Guy wore a faint grin, "I suddenly thought, if you sent me to prison you'd have to come too. It's against the law to let anyone under sixteen years of age have a shotgun of his own."

None of us needed to be reminded that Father had given Guy the gun, at a time when there was a veritable plague of hawks threatening every feathered creature on the farm. Hawks are terrible birds and sworn enemies of every farmer, but we didn't think that would be excuse enough to keep Father out of prison. We were sure he didn't think so, either.

So the matter was closed. We scattered happily, secure in the knowledge that justice must not only be done, it must be seen to be done.

XII

Gentle Jesus

Time had slipped around again to the Sunday when we might expect the visiting minister from one or other of the churches. Everything was immaculate inside the house and out, and we youngsters wore our best bib-and-tucker, whatever that means. I had only one small blot on my conscience — I'd lost the sixpence Mother had armed us with for the collection plate.

We all knew this munificence was a sort of insurance. We were giving to God, Mother said. It was Granny who added a rider to that. She worked it out that if we treated God right by giving money to His church, He'd treat us right in return at such times as we called on Him for help.

So I'd placed myself in a pretty precarious position, losing my church money. A vulnerable position. It would be a fat lot of good yelling for help I hadn't even paid for.

Also, I wasn't going to be able to get away with pretending I was putting a sixpence in the collection plate when Father took it round. His eyes were too sharp for that.

I stood back and was the last into the big room where the church services were held, but even so the problem was still with me, unsolved. I could have asked Mother for another sixpence but it hardly seemed fair to me that she should have to pay twice for my place in God's graces. Besides, none of us kids were absolutely above suspicion. I couldn't overlook the fact that I had once taken two peppermints when the understanding was quite definite that I should take only one. Mother had been grieved over my deceit, my lies about the peppermint. How would she feel if she believed I was secretly pocketing the sixpence I'd lost?

So in the end I went into the church room without a penny. It didn't help in the least to find it was the Hellfire-and-damnation preacher this Sunday. He was not likely to put in a good word up above for any of us, especially not us children. He never had forgotten or forgiven us for something we were really innocent of, a handful of hideous, loathsome weta insects in the guest room where he was to have slept that night.

It was unfair of him to blame us for his fright; we didn't mean them for him. We meant them for the noxious weeds inspector, a man who seemed to us youngsters to be Father's most deadly enemy. Father was always irritable after the inspector's visit and would march belligerently about the farm for days afterwards chopping exaggeratedly at tiny plants of blackberry or gorse and muttering about people who could not mind their own business. What harm was a bit of gorse doing on a man's land, anyway? Down in the South Island the farmers had miles of gorse hedges and they didn't have Government inspectors poking a nose in and telling them to get rid of six-inch-high plants of gorse! Noxious weeds, indeed!

Anyway, that was the man we meant the wetas for. Gosh, we would have been stupid to play a trick on the parson, our insurance agent, so to speak. He wasn't fond of children at the best of times. He wasn't actually fond of anybody.

And he never believed a word we young folk said to him. Even when we went to the trouble of walking him round Father's garden he said we should know better than to pull his leg and lie to him. The trouble was he'd never seen or even heard of egg-plants. I suppose he did feel a bit of an idiot, starting to tell us where eggs really do come from.

Also, being a city man born and bred, he never did believe we could catch mullet by merely rowing along in the reeds lining the riverbanks. We wanted to take him out with us some night and make him eat his words but he wouldn't even give us satisfaction.

Oh, well. Poor man. I suppose his mother liked him even though no one else seemed to. He had a lovely singing voice, like a choirboy's tenor, except that he warbled like mad on the high top notes. It was fun to watch his Adam's apple jumping about in his throat when he reached the loud parts of the hymns.

"You're not paying attention," my elder sister chided me in an ultra-pious whisper. She was making sure she got in good with God. Fair enough. If the parson wasn't prepared to stand up for us we'd have to look after our own interests.

The first hymn was halfway through. Most of the congregation were singing but some were just opening and shutting their lips. Father always did this, he couldn't sing a note. Mother was playing the piano and singing too. There was absolutely nothing in the world Mother couldn't do, all of us kids knew that. She only had to put her cool fingers on our heads and she could even make headaches better.

I forgot about the hymn and just stood there, looking at Mother. Her pretty brown hair was even more wavy than usual, there was a nice pink colour in her cheeks and her brown eyes looked like the oak table when it was just polished. She was wearing a brown silk dress with lots of small tucks in the blouse and tiny brown buttons all down the front. I remembered her saying the dress was really getting old-fashioned but Father liked her to wear it. Her fingers on the piano keys were delicate white and hardly looked strong enough to carry the two rings.

She had been very ill a while back but God had pulled her through to health again. I hoped she would live to be 120 years old, and I would die when I was ninety. I thought I'd worked that out right. Mother was thirty when I was born, Granny said, so that way she and I would get off to Heaven together...

"Sit down!" Someone was tugging at the hem of my dress. "The hymn's finished, dreamy-head!"

Next would be the lesson for the day. I'd better concentrate on that or be sent from the room. He was talking about Jesus. "Gentle Jesus, meek and mild, look upon a little child..."

He wasn't saying that, though. He was reading from the Bible. "...one of the soldiers with a spear pierced His side, and forthwith came thereout blood and water..."

Not Jesus! I saw a calf once — it had fallen onto a sharp stake and it was bleeding from its side — oh, please God, not Jesus! Meek and mild... "Pity my simplicity..."

I could still remember when I was quite little and something made me frightened, or perhaps the grown-ups closed the hall door and there was no light at all in my room — I'd run through all the hymns I knew until I found one warm and comforting — and of course it was nearly always a Jesus hymn.

• • • • •

"...came thereout blood and water..."

"You're not listening," my sister hissed, and I poked out my tongue at her. "I don't want to listen."

Understanding, my sister whispered, "It gets better later on. He'll come to the part where Jesus rises from the dead..."

Father turned his head. "Stop talking, you two."

Stop talking and listen to gentle Jesus being killed...

In *Grimm's Fairy Tales* it was always a giant who killed people, or they got lost or were eaten by bears. Hans Andersen's fairy tales changed people into witches or wolves or something. *Gulliver's Travels* told how you could be tiny as tiny one minute and then blow up into someone as big as the Michelin tyre man. It was awful to wake up in the night and be too frightened to even look at your hands in case they had gone as small as a doll's hand or as big as an elephant's foot. But they never did, so perhaps the story about Jesus wasn't true, either? He never did get a spear stuck into His side...

Strengthened by this thought I began to listen again. "...and they worshipped Him, and returned to Jerusalem with great joy. And they were continually in the temple, praising and blessing God. Amen."

It wasn't true about Jesus. Great joy, the parson said! They wouldn't have great joy if Jesus was dead. It was just a story.

I wished the parson had explained in the first place it was just a story, I wouldn't have felt so sick in my tummy. That calf, the one that fell on a stake...

"Now we will sing together hymn number 168. 'Now just a word for Jesus, Your dearest friend so true...'"

This was more like it. The whole thing had been only a stupid nightmare. I sang my guts out, as the boys said later. Mother looked across the piano at me and smiled. She was having nothing to do with spears and things. She couldn't even bear to catch a fish on a hook.

The sermon was short and not nearly so Hell-fire as usual, thank goodness. The dinner cooking itself slowly in the oven smelt good.

But then the minister said, "I think we'll have the young folk stay back for communion. There has to be a first time even if they just sit quietly and watch." So he moved away to the white table with the white lace cloth where Mother had set out the tiny glasses and everything. I didn't mind a bit having to stay back, it wouldn't take long and anyway I was still warm with happiness over Jesus not being killed after all.

The minister took the cover off the table and stood with his back to us but I couldn't see what he was doing. Then he turned round and came across to Mother first, and he said, "This is the body and blood of Jesus Christ…" and he stood there and made Mother eat it.

Made her!! Flesh and blood — gentle Jesus, meek and mild — I thought I was going to be sick…

I was lying on the couch in the other room when I opened my eyes and Mother was saying, "She faints easily — and it really is hot indoors today."

Granny made the impatient clicking noise with her tongue. "Tch, tch! Can't you see what's the matter with the child? Why don't you tell her the sacrament is not for real, it's only a promise we won't hurt Jesus like they did on the cross?"

Dimly, I saw what she meant but I still wished the parson would not use exactly those words. It's hard for young children to understand the beauty behind what's actually said.

· · · · ·

XIII

Noxious weed inspector

Although Father did try to correct our habit of referring to our official visitor as the "noxious inspector" I suspect he was secretly in agreement with the uncomplimentary title. There could surely be no true rapport between these two; one living in a world of rules and regulations, the other slaving his life out on a pioneer-type five hundred acre farm.

There was in fact open antagonism between them. "I see you still have that gorse bush on the headland," the inspector might begin on a mild note. "I suppose you do remember my ordering you to have it rooted out?"

"Ordering?" Father's tell-tale moustache twitched. "I believe you did mention it," he said, keeping steadily on with the job in hand. The rhythmic swish, swish of milk being squirted into a tin bucket almost drowned out his voice.

The inspector's eyes bored into the back of Father's head. "Well?" he said, and waited. And seemed likely to wait. The milking went steadily on.

"I'll expect to see that gorse cleared before my next visit," the inspector tried again, not quite so mildly. "If I find it still there you really will be in trouble. I'm warning you."

"I'll dig it out when I get time," Father promised, but we were left with the distinct impression he wouldn't be likely to have a spare moment this side of the millennium. And of course the gorse was still there in all its golden, sweet-scented glory when the inspector made his next call some months later.

This time the two men had a flaming row. Law court proceedings were mentioned by both parties to the quarrel, Father maintaining that the inspector had no legal right to set foot on another man's land and the inspector being equally emphatic about the rights of a Government Inspector who was hampered in his work by uncooperative farmers of dubious intelligence and even more doubtful integrity.

Fortunately Mother happened to come into the room at that point and as Father never willingly forfeited her good opinion the matter was temporarily dropped, apart from a few muttered words from each of the men as they parted at the door.

"He seems a nice man," Mother made the remark in all innocence. She hadn't heard what was going on. "Did he say anything about that dreadful tree with the poisonous leaves and berries?"

"The tutu tree? No, he didn't," Father looked thoughtful, and no wonder. In spite of every effort on his part, the farm was riddled with the most noxious weed of them all, pretty, shrub-tall tutu trees. The curse of the North, Father named it.

We knew all about tutu, we'd seen cows blow up as big as an elephant and die after eating even a small portion of the tutu leaves. You could save them, Father said, if you caught them in time and thrust a knife between their ribs. He said it was the gases in their tummies that killed them, which verdict upset us kids considerably. Granny's favourite warning was not to drink the fizzy soda water and bottled lemonade we loved unless we really wanted to fill our poor stomachs with gases. We decided we might take more notice of her in future. The prospect of having a knife thrust between our ribs held surprisingly little appeal.

"He didn't mention the tutu," Father puzzled. It would seem the comparatively harmless gorse bush had blinded the zealous inspector to more important duties. "So why," Father added, "is he persecuting me over one small gorse bush?"

'Persecuting'? I loved a new word but I wasn't sure what this one meant. It was Mother who supplied the answer. She said, "I doubt if the inspector enjoys his visits any more than you do, Norman. It's a big question, dear. I sometimes dare to wonder exactly why God sees fit to allow the growth of deadly noxious weeds."

Father muttered something about noxious weed inspectors being allowed to flourish unchallenged by the Almighty, but I was no longer interested in the adults' conversation. My mind was occupied with the new word.

From what Mother said I knew the word persecuting meant

visiting. I felt I could work the new word in impressively next essay at school. Something like, "we are glad our friends come persecuting us quite often." Or, "my mother has gone persecuting our neighbours again today." I thought I might get pretty high marks from the teachers.

But with teachers one never knows. I remembered our letter-writing lesson last week. We youngsters had been taught to end our letters with the reassuring words, "I remain, your loving niece," or whatever the relationship might be. This seemed all right to me until in one of my more lucid moments I looked the word up in the dictionary.

I suppose most children are show-offs in one way or another. I thought it would boost my image considerably in the teacher's eyes if I used the dictionary. So I stopped chewing the end of my pencil and began laboriously to write. "…I am what's left over, your loving niece…"

I spent some time explaining to the teacher that's what the dictionary had said 'remain' means but she was not amused. I guess it was a case of giving a dog a bad name. I'd already had a sharp taste of the cane that morning for talking to my brother. I felt this was unfair. It wasn't my fault he sat five desks away from me.

I made up my mind to ask the noxious inspector next time we met why he didn't come persecuting us at school. He'd find great patches of stinging nettles flourishing just through the school fence. That should interest him.

Cattle died hideously if they ate stinging nettles. In some ways it was worse than tutu. If we chanced to stand on a branch of tutu with our bare feet nothing happened, but if we stood on stinging nettles we were away from school for a week with poisoned feet. Some of the boys kicked their football into the nettles. To them, swollen feet were pretty bad but school was worse. It seemed the only way to get a week off. Although the noxious inspector's visits to our home were memorable occasions for all of us he didn't come by so very often. About once in three months, which was quite attentive of him when one considers the huge area he had to patrol.

Father felt there might be others in the district equally worthy of his attentions. That great spread of Californian thistles up-river a mile or two, what was he doing about that? Foxgloves, too, beautiful but deadly. There were plenty of foxgloves about, Father pointed out, if only the inspector could bring himself to bypass our gorse bush and concentrate on the sins and omissions of others. He never would, of course. We knew he'd never pass us by in his launch as long as that cheeky gorse bush stood there on the riverbank. The worst kind of noxious weed, he called it, and again that seemed unfair. Cattle didn't die if they ate gorse.

We'd finally got round to looking up the word 'noxious' in the dictionary and learned that it meant harmful and unwholesome. If gorse was harmful and unwholesome, what about the karaka tree? It wasn't even declared noxious, yet the berries were known to be deadly poisonous. We talked about our friends who had been crippled by the eating of karaka tree berries. When these young men were small children they found a tree of the tempting orange coloured berries and would certainly have died shortly after eating them if the Maoris had not rescued the lads. It was said the Maoris buried them in sand up to their chins and this saved their lives. Even so, their limbs were twisted and misshapen for life, such was the power of the innocent-looking berries.

Father did his best to teach us at an early age which berries were poisonous and which were not, but I think he would have been horrified if he'd known how many of the unlisted species we hogged into. We made whole meals of prune-sized, tangy taraire berries. The fruit of the tall native fuchsias, too, and wild cape gooseberries were a great delicacy. At least, we thought the golden cape gooseberries were native plants but they probably began their spread from some farmer's bought grass seed.

Hinau berries, or pigeonwood, or the beautiful scarlet and black berries of the kahikatea and the totara trees, no. We didn't know for sure whether or not these were poisonous but in any case we lost interest when we tasted them. They were horrible. We could have understood the inspector taking a set against these berries, unwholesome or not.

He had just been around on one of his controversial visits when tragedy struck our farm. Father's best Jersey cow decided to try for herself whether the tutu berries and leaves really were poisonous.

She was too far gone before Father found her. Worse, she left behind in this vale of tears a lovely little two-day-old heifer calf. It fell to my lot to look after the little creature.

Most calves are hard to teach how to drink out of a bucket. The teacher almost always ends up covered in milk from head to toe, not to mention trampled feet and the nails chewed half off the fingers offered to the slobbering young animal.

Still, I was accustomed to this rather oblique form of gratitude. Young Buttercup and I were great friends in no time at all. I was giving the calf its midday drink when I heard the familiar and easily recognisable putt-putt of the inspector's launch.

Father and the boys had heard it too. They came down to the wharf paddock to greet the visitor, Father's eyes already shooting blue fire.

"What's he doing back here already? It's only three days since his last visit! I'll write to the Prime Minister about this..."

"I think he's going past," someone announced. "He's probably hunting foxgloves."

Father didn't seem to appreciate our hunting calls and squeals of laughter. I think we all caught his uneasy glance in the direction of the gorse bush. I began to feel a bit sick... Perhaps they could take Father off to prison? "A gorse bush is a serious offence," the inspector had said more than once.

I breathed a sigh of relief when the launch went past our wharf and continued on up the river. But the inspector must have seen us there in the river paddock, he turned the launch and came swirling back.

The quarrel was nothing new, except that this time both men got onto a bitter personal note. I don't suppose Father enjoyed being called an obstinate old Pommy any more than the inspector approved of his new title, a white-collared desk pigeon.

We kids tried to keep out of the row and for once in our lives had nothing to say even to each other. It was my calf, Buttercup, which upset the applecart, as the saying goes. I honestly didn't let go the rope on purpose. And anyway, how could I have known the stupid little critter would rush between the inspector's feet?

I think even Father, his sworn enemy, was a bit appalled when he saw the inspector lying flat on his back in the long grass and deep mud of a cow paddock. At least the visitor's fury was turned in another direction. I'd had some lectures and some pretty pointed scoldings in my short lifetime but the blast I got from this gentleman was something quite new. Some of the words I didn't even understand, I'd never heard them before. It wasn't much good trying to pick up any fascinating new words, either, he spoke too quickly.

"Grab the calf's rope, you stupid child!" Father took a hand in the situation. "And make sure it doesn't slip off over its head."

I fell on the rope and clung to it with an iron grip nothing, not even death itself, would loosen. The inspector had risen from his muddy repose and was scraping muck and rubbish from the trousers of his expensive-looking suit. He was standing right in our way but I didn't let go of the rope again even when Buttercup decided to go one side of him and I the other.

The rope tightened behind his knees. Between the two of us, Buttercup and me, we ran him a hundred yards before he sat down hard on the grass. For our next involuntary trick we dragged him round the paddock on his seat, the rope hopelessly tangled with his legs. I hadn't known a calf's neck muscles could be so strong.

When everything eventually sorted itself out, more or less, and Father's offer to have the jagged rips in the inspector's trousers mended had been sharply turned down, I found myself once more on the mat.

The inspector snapped, "Why is that beast here anyway? And why didn't you let go of the rope? If I thought you'd arranged this..."

"Oh no, I didn't," I was starting to blubber and sniffle unmusically. "It's my pet calf, I was just feeding it."

He still looked suspicious. It wasn't any comfort to know Father shared in his mistrust. "And why, if this is not a trick, is the animal not out with the other calves?"

"It's too little." Even a white collar desk pigeon should have known that. Still, after what had happened I suppose he couldn't be blamed for thinking the calf was pretty strong.

He said, "Well, why not leave it with its mother? Isn't that the customary thing to do?"

He'd addressed the question to Father but I took it upon myself to explain. "Buttercup's mother is dead, you see. She ate tutu and blew up and died."

"She did?" It was easy to see the inspector had suddenly cheered up. He turned back to Father and said mildly, "And where on your farm might I expect to find enough tutu to kill a full-grown cow?"

My brothers were looking daggers at me. "Nitwit, giving the show away —"

"Well?" the inspector prompted Father. "Where is this poisonous noxious weed growing? And why haven't I been told of it?"

The man must be crazy, no one would deliberately lead him to a noxious weed. But Father was answering him patiently. "It's nothing, a mere plant or two out the back of the farm. You know how it is with tutu, I'm forever chopping away at it —"

A plant or two? Oh, boy. We held our breath. If the inspector chose to inspect the area Father had tried so hard and so unsuccessfully to clear — oh boy!

The visitor seemed to hesitate. The sun was beating down mercilessly, striking heat waves from the rocky scoria ground he would have to traverse to get to the back of the farm. He glanced at his watch and said, "Hmm. Well, I have an appointment up the river. But next time I'm up this way…" The threat hung in mid-air as he climbed into his launch and left.

Father watched him go. Then, while we scampered about the paddock playing tig with the calf he, Father, went striding away up to the house. We were somehow not at all surprised to see him making his way towards the gorse bush with an axe in his hands.

XIV

A small miracle

It seemed strange to me that our Friend had suddenly turned His back on me so completely. Life was definitely going against me. For one thing I'd made an utter fool of myself at the school concert. Given a few lines to say which should in my opinion at least have brought forth a standing ovation, I blew the whole scene. The touching little recitation came out like this.

"Life-is-mostly-froth-and-bubble-Two-things-stand-out-like-stone-Kindness-in-another's-trouble-Courage-in-your-own-Can-I-sit-down-now-please?" The speed at which it was delivered would have won the Derby, no trouble at all. Stage fright is a devastating thing, especially as it doesn't really strike until that enormous sea of faces (three dozen people at least) stretches out there below you.

Added to that I'd gone off and hidden myself in the caves for twenty-four hours. A business acquaintance of Father's was visiting us. He was plump and good-natured and very fond of children — and I hated him. Or perhaps feared him is the right word. He had a habit of saying with monotonous frequency, "I'm going to take you home with me and you can live on boiled lollies all day long. How's that for a pretty little girl?"

I didn't like boiled lollies, they made my teeth ache, and I didn't want to go to Auckland with him, I wanted to stay with Mother. So every time he came to see Father on mill business I was AWOL when he took his leave. But this time he was still there having a cup of tea with Father when I sneaked back to the house. He'd left his departure too late, the tide had gone out too far. There wouldn't be enough water in the river to float his launch for hours and hours yet.

And of course he had to take me on his kindly old knee and say, "Well, are you ready to come home with me? Get her clothes packed, Granny. She's coming on the big steamer with me all the way to Auckland."

I had the presence of mind to snatch a couple of peanut biscuits as I slipped away through the kitchen, not very much to stand between me and starvation but they would be better than nothing. I meant to spin them out until I appeared at the breakfast table next morning. But then I thought there might be rats in the cave and if they found out I had biscuits down there — oh boy!

So I ate them as I slipped through the trees and bracken fern towards the caves. I'd never been down into the caves by myself but with the sun streaming down and birds singing all round me I was comfortably sure I wouldn't be too terribly scared. It never entered my head they would be worried about me at home.

What a night that was! Rustlings and every odd kind of shuffling noise under the sun — if there had been any sun. It was pitch black darkness down there and of course I hadn't thought to grab matches to light the candles we'd stuck on the rocks some time before. I spent the night absolutely petrified, not moving a finger and hardly daring even to breathe. The mad things kids do! I was too terrified to stay in the cave and too terrified to leave it in the dark. Besides, if I did manage to find my way home the visitor might still be there and the whole come-with-me business would start up all over again.

I passed the time by bawling at the top of my voice, until it suddenly struck me there could be devils or something lurking in the other parts of the cave and my yelling would be certain to attract them. Or wolves. Or even some of Father's ghosts.

It must have been almost morning when I quite unintentionally fell asleep. When I crept out into the daylight and the warmth of the late afternoon sun it was comforting to know that the boiled-lolly man would have gone home by now, that was for sure.

It was, I think, the only time in my life I was given an honest to goodness, no nonsense smacked bottom. Still, even that was better than having to leave Mother and go and live on boiled lollies until I was grey-haired and had take-out teeth like Granny.

But that was not the end of my troubles. I didn't altogether blame God for letting Father sell my heifer. It was a long time since Father had given me the day-old calf and told me I could have it if I could manage to rear it, and if Father himself had forgotten it really belonged to me — well, I guessed God had an awful lot more on His mind than Father had.

Father honestly did forget Black Velvet belonged to me. When the boys found me encouraging her to jump the sales paddock fence and take off to the far end of the farm and they went and told Father she was the calf he'd given me, he couldn't believe it was the same animal.

After all, Black Velvet had been running more or less wild with the other young cattle out the back of the farm for two years. I wouldn't have recognised her myself if I hadn't made a point of keeping in touch with her, so to speak. I'd been taking it for granted she was mine and what's more her first calf would in a legal sort of way belong to me, also.

The boys came back to me with a sound business proposition. Let Father sell Black Velvet, who was a beautiful, streamlined, elegant young lady and would fetch a lot of money, then I could persuade Father she really was mine and I could have all the money. Or even share it with them if I felt that way inclined.

I managed to convince them I didn't want the money, I wanted to keep Black Velvet, and this seemed to irritate them quite surprisingly. All that money turned down! They told me rather coldly it was fair enough letting Father sell her and divide up the money because she couldn't expect to hang round the farm eating her head off for another year and giving nothing back in return. She wasn't going to be milking this year at all.

I was angry. Just because Black Velvet had decided not to have a calf this year she had to be sold and might even be sent to the Freezing Works! There was no justice in this. I hated the crowd of them, including Father, almost.

We had a young fellow from down South staying with us at the time. I think he was supposed to be training as a farm cadet. He was only about sixteen but tall for his age and seemed much older, especially as his voice had already taken on the deep masculine tones of an adult.

I was gratified that he, Ronald, shared my sense of outrage. He said it was a lousy trick to sell my heifer, but even this warm support was not much help. He offered to go and tell Father this was in truth my own day-old calf grown up, but then we remembered he'd never set eyes on Black Velvet in his life before so how could he identify her?

I would have resorted to my habit of turning the problem over to God, except that it seemed a bit sneaky to go behind Father's back and ask God to let me have my own way. Besides, I doubted if He could do much about it at this late stage.

Time was running out. The sale had been set down for next Wednesday and already Father's surplus stock was gathered together ready for the auctioneer's visit. Notices had gone out to all those interested in buying and quite a crowd was expected. Preparations went ahead for feeding them on sandwiches, plain cakes and strong black tea.

Cattle sales were mystifying performances. It sounded to me as though the auctioneer was amusing himself and annoying everyone else by shouting, "Hip! Runawayrunawayrunaway — hip! That man over there..." I knew the customers were annoyed, they shouted right back at him during the whole transaction.

We youngsters were told to keep out of the way so we perched ourselves on the top of a gate nearby and settled down to enjoy the fun of the fair. Except that I was in no mood to enjoy anything very much. I had eyes for no animal but my own sleek black heifer, bunched as she was among a huddle of other dry stock — meaning cows which were not milking and not intending to do so that year. This sale could have been hilarious if I hadn't been so upset about Black Velvet. All sorts of funny things happened, like the look on a farmer's face when he found he had accidentally bought two dozen ducks in place of the large crate of silky-black young pigs he'd understood the man to be auctioning. Then when the pigs were sold someone rather stupidly allowed them to escape, so that proceedings were held up while the crowd scattered in all directions, hotly pursuing nimble little shrieking, squealing piglets.

After that exhausting episode lunch was served on long trestle tables. The sandwiches were soft and fresh and tasted good. So did the sweet, hot tea, but there was subdued grumbling over the absence of beer. I made up my mind to ask someone tomorrow what the word 'wowser' meant. If Father was a wowser it must mean something quite complimentary, I thought.

Ronald was with us kids for lunch. Because he was supposed to be learning farming he'd been moving among the crowd all morning lending a helping hand with this and that. We'd hardly set eyes upon him since breakfast, which was a pity. His ready sympathy would have helped me through the ordeal of Black Velvet's departure.

Father was still convinced we were mistaken about this heifer being Black Velvet. He said she was a different colour from the miserable, sickly little calf he'd given me. This was true; two years of luxuriant living on the lush green hills at the back of the farm had darkened her coat and given it a lovely sheen one might never have expected the calf to develop. Some of the more scrawny young heifers — yes. Any one of them could have been the adult counterpart of that calf. But, Father insisted, not the one I'd picked out.

Oh, well. It was too late now, anyway. Black Velvet would be coming up for auction very soon. I began to cry but had the sense to keep down the volume of my grief. A bawling youngster would have been packed off out of there smartly.

Father must have glimpsed my misery. He came across to the gate where we sat. With, I suppose, justifiable irritation he said, "Take that sulky look off your face, my girl. I know what's wrong but you're mistaken — that heifer isn't yours. All the same…"

I thought he had weakened and was about to say he wouldn't sell her but instead he said, "I tell you what I'll do. Seeing you're so miserable about the animal I'll see that you get at least half the money when she's sold. All right? I couldn't make a fairer offer than that, could I?"

Ungratefully, I said nothing. I didn't even nod my head. It wasn't the money I wanted. I just sat there, mulishly silent.

Father flared at me, "Don't be stupid! That heifer will fetch a good price. You'd be a lucky little girl to have that much money in the Post Office."

He strode away and in due time the bidding for Black Velvet began. As Father had expected, she brought a higher price than most of her age group. A man at the back of the crowd of bidders ran the price up and finally succeeded in getting her. It was only a matter of minutes now until she'd be led onto one of the pontoons and taken away down river to the buyer's farm. Unless of course the man was staying on to bid for other cattle.

Apparently he was. Black Velvet was left waiting in the sale yard. She was still waiting there when all the other animals had been claimed and taken away. By then the crowd was dwindling, almost everyone had taken their purchases and left the scene.

It was only when we were alone with the auctioneer Father awoke to the fact that Black Velvet was not going to be claimed. He had a tiff with the auctioneer over it but neither of them could come up with any explanation.

"You sold the animal, man!" Father stormed. "You should be able to identify the bidder."

"Are you kidding?" The auctioneer's temper was rising. "How was I to know the man wasn't going to come forward and claim the wretched beast? It's hard enough to pick who is actually bidding in a crowd like this — and anyway, you heard the bids. You know the people round here better than I do, I'm a stranger in the district."

Those mightn't have been his actual words, it's a long time ago, but that was the gist of what he said. Father was pretty annoyed over the way things had turned out but there was nothing he could do other than let Black Velvet go back to her life of ease and luxury out the back of the farm. Next year she would have a calf for sure, so here she was back with us for the rest of her life.

Ronald and I were on the wharf fishing for eels after tea that evening. "Lucky thing about your heifer. I guess you're happy you've still got her here on the farm?"

He seemed puzzled over the whole thing and so was I, but I had a feeling my Friend had worked the miracle somehow. Almost as though he'd read my thoughts, Ronald said, "You're a funny little brat, you know. I bet you're giving that Almighty of yours all the credit. What d'you think He did, choke that chap that bought Black Velvet, or drown him, or something? The chap didn't turn up, did he?"

I shook my head. "I don't suppose he ever will, either. Who do you reckon was bidding?"

"Don't you know?"

I shook my head again. "All we could hear was a deep voice calling out the price he wanted to give."

"Like this?" Ronald said, and began bidding for an imaginary animal. His voice was very deep and adult.

Early transport – or was it sport – in the Hokianga

XV

Not without incident

Big flap. Dentist Day had come round again. We said it wasn't a year since our last visit but the calendar proved us wrong. The dentist himself had the last word, bless him. Business must have been slack at that time, we were sure no dentist in his right mind would welcome to his surgery almost a couple of dozen grizzling and sullen little monsters all to be attended to in one short day.

It usually fell to Father's lot to get out his big passenger launch and, calling at almost every homestead along the way, gather together the long-faced young martyrs and deliver them to the one and only dentist at Kohukohu.

There can't have been much fun for the parents accompanying their children on the tumbril-like trip across the harbour and through the Narrows to the township.

Coming back was worse. Even the brightest and bravest grin had vanished behind gory handkerchiefs. The whole launch reeked of the pseudo-painkilling drug, cocaine. The only bright spot for us youngsters was the lively quarrel which inevitably developed on the way home.

Through stiff, numbed lips we would declare war on those favoured few who merely had to have fillings done and were trading on their good fortune by jeering at us. Their use of a descriptive adjective for the state of our mouths shocked our Puritanical souls deeply. We were not unfamiliar with the offending word as used round the farm in times of great stress but that was different. The worst of it was we couldn't accuse them of swearing — they were after all only telling the truth, our mouths were *bloody* in the correct sense of the word. All the same, it was only by good fortune they were not bloody-mouths themselves.

Oh, well. They got back as good as they gave even though our retaliation had to be dealt out discreetly in view of our sore mouths and the fact our parents were aboard the launch. A slap in the face would have hurt us much more than it would the aggressors with nothing worse than fillings in their mouths.

Our yearly visits to the dentist were not without incident, humorous or otherwise. We sometimes even found our philosophy of life being tested. On one occasion a sudden wild storm struck our neighbour's smallish craft when he was negotiating one of the most treacherous spots imaginable, the rip-race stretch of water separating northern Hokianga from the southern areas. The Narrows, wickedly turbulent at times and, the Maoris declared, bottomless. At least, the depth of water had never been fathomed.

Our squabbling was forgotten as we banded together in a suicide pact of loyalty. If any of us were to drown we'd all drown together. Not that we had much choice in the matter, if the storm continued its ferocity we'd drown anyway, loyalty pact or no loyalty pact.

"Who's talking about drowning?" The launch owner turned his head to throw us a flashing grin. "Of course, if you want to take a dip you're welcome, but no one's drowning in my launch, thanks all the same."

Take a dip in that wild sea? We entered into the joke, giggling appreciatively in spite of the strain on our mouths. Everyone on board knew we'd have a fat chance of emerging alive from a plunge into the waters of the Narrows. Besides, said one young wit, we didn't have our bathing togs with us. It wouldn't be quite the thing to drown yourself without first donning your togs.

As the storm worsened we were near to drowning, the lot of us, driver and all. It was only through his skill and level-headed manoeuvring of the pitching, tossing launch that we made it back to calmer waters. For almost an hour our fate had been in the balance.

The driver kept joking with us even when he must surely have been fighting sheer panic. The responsibility for so many young lives was entirely his, the launch was not big enough to allow parents aboard this trip.

We went putt-putting up the river to his first port of call. Parents were waiting on the wharf to collect their young folk. "What sort of time did you have in the Narrows?" The father seemed a bit worried.

"Pretty rough, was it?"

"Not bad," said our chaperone, "It got a bit nippy in places but there was no danger." Oh, brother! We kids grinned wryly at each other. There was danger all right. It was only thanks to him we were there at all.

Our house was the last, the other children living down-river from our farm, so he came up to the house for a cup of tea. The tale of the storm lost nothing from the way we youngsters told it. This time we were not allowing him to play down his part in the drama.

Granny kept going "tch-tch" with her lips all through the story, a habit of hers when she was really shocked. She said, "Well, did you ever hear the like! You could all have been drowned. I thank God you came through the storm safe and well."

Her enthusiasm vaguely surprised us. We'd always felt sure she looked upon us as a disfiguring blot upon the landscape of her declining years. Life could have been much more simple for her had we all been swept away to a watery grave.

Father's thanksgiving was not quite so unexpected. "It would be most fitting if we were all to bow our heads and give thanks to Almighty God right here and now," he said.

"If you'll excuse me…" Our guest — our hero! — rose to his feet and picked up his oilskin coat. "I'll be getting along." He shared a genial smile among us all, then left rather abruptly.

It was only after he'd gone Mother spoke up. "I have no doubt he felt it would have been more appropriate to thank him, Norman. Have you forgotten he doesn't share our religious beliefs? He doesn't believe there is an Almighty God."

"What he does or doesn't believe is no concern of mine," Father sounded snappy. He never liked to have Mother differ from him, even ever so slightly.

Tucked up in front of the fire with warm red flannel strips round our swelling faces, we youngsters held a court of enquiry and possible judgement upon the young man in question. True, it would be awful not to believe we had a Friend to help us. But after all, his unbelief meant the launch driver had rescued us all absolutely under his own steam with no assistance from the Almighty or anyone else. Our respectful admiration knew no bounds. Even with the help of the Almighty we could never have pulled off such a magnificent feat.

Our next visit to the dentist began uneventfully. The sun was shining, the harbour glassy smooth and not a cloud in the sky. Father's big launch *Eureka* was strong and sturdy and blunt-nosed enough to sneer at any sudden storm. Mother went along with us as chaperone or nurse or what-have-you for the whole crowd, thus setting other mothers free to get on with their jam-making or preserving or whatever pressing duties they had.

On board, too, were a few outsiders prepared to pay a small fare for the privilege of transport to Kohukohu and back. One large middle-aged woman fascinated us children, she was so smiling and good-natured. Most of our journey was taken up learning how to make paper hats and sailing ships. She even taught us the art of fashioning charming little frogs out of our handkerchiefs.

The knowledge that our new-found friend would be a passenger on the launch going home brightened our visit to the dentist, though my own good spirits sank when I heard the dentist telling Mother he was darned if he was prepared to struggle with those molars, I'd have to be given chloroform this time. I supposed he wanted me asleep so that he could help himself to my teeth in peace, sort of.

Fair enough. Granny had often stressed the dangers of chloroform but if my time had come to die I might as well be choked to death as go any other way.

To my surprise I didn't get the chloroform after all. A doctor was called in to administer it but he refused to put me to sleep. There was a hurried whispering consultation with the dentist, then they came back and gave me a good doing with an unpleasantly cold stethoscope pressed over the region of my nervously thudding heart.

They went away and talked to Mother and Father. I wasn't trying to listen but I couldn't help catching the words, "too risky," and something about even a young tomboy could have a faulty heart, you know. I could see Mother was upset about something, she had set her lips in the bright and brittle smile which never did deceive any of us. We always knew when she was worried.

Anyway, I didn't have to have my teeth out after all. All the same, I wasn't happy. There was a disquieting thought preying on my mind, something I could have asked Mother about if I'd had the courage.

On the way home in the launch I was glad I was sitting close by Mother with her arm about my shoulders, because our bright and genial frog-making lady friend suddenly gave up muttering to herself and drinking out of a brown bottle and rushed out of the cabin.

A yell of anger from Father brought us all out to see what was happening. She'd grabbed the sharp-pointed pike-pole and was trying to shove Father overboard — had almost succeeded in doing so. Perhaps she didn't know he couldn't swim and moreover he was the only person aboard capable of running the launch engine and steering us through the intricacies of the winding river's course.

From what little sense we could get out of her she'd come to the conclusion that even the paltry, token fare Father had charged her was too much. She would have preferred to spend the couple of bob at the pub.

Between the lot of us we got her back into the cabin. The launch began to swing in a wide circle as Father left the steering wheel unattended long enough to slam the cabin doors and lock them on the outside. We heard him clambering back over the cabin to his post in the engine room up ahead. I don't suppose any of us were particularly happy but it was the only possible arrangement.

Fortunately our inebriated friend forgot her grievance against Father and decided to enliven the rest of the journey home by singing at the top of her not inconsiderable voice. Mother couldn't stop her — I must say we kids learned a lot we didn't know before during that two-hour trip. The songs she was singing had nothing to do with Moody & Sankey.

Far from holding a grudge against Father, she seemed to take a fancy to him as we neared her home. She wouldn't leave the launch and when he tried to make her step on to the wharf she grabbed him and gave him such a smacking kiss on the cheek he must have been almost deafened.

The fact that Mother was biting her lips to hide her amusement and the launchful of kids were quite uproarious didn't seem to improve poor Father's state of mind. When he finally got her landed on terra firma she walked across the wharf and fell into the river.

The situation was no longer funny. Even if Father could swim he'd need a crane to lift her from the water. We held back our laughter until we saw she could swim like a — well, let's say like a whale — and was making for the shore. She even managed to turn her dripping head and shout a loving and slightly less blurred farewell to our paternal ancestor.

We didn't get on our way immediately. Father found her bag of groceries on the cabin and was forced to take them to her as she waddled damply along the wharf to meet him. We felt free to let our laughter break as we saw him drop the groceries on the wharf and make a beeline back to the security of the launch. Our trip to the dentist had turned into a fun thing after all.

I was almost ready for bed that evening when I remembered what had been bothering me on the way back from the dentist's. Mother would have to be told sooner or later so I decided to get it over with. I went back, crying, to the living room.

Mother managed to extract the information that it was something the doctor had said. She and Father exchanged glances and she said quickly, "So you did hear what we were talking about. My goodness, you do have sharp ears for a little girl of eight years, don't you?" She was making light of it.

"There's nothing to worry yourself about," Father said, "Lots and lots of people can't take chloroform, you know."

"It wasn't that," I bawled, "It — it was what the doctor said..."

They must have thought I was crying over the faulty heart part of it but that didn't bother me a scrap. I guess I didn't understand the implications. Oh, no. It was something much more worrying than that.

I stood there rubbing my eyes and sniffling until Father quite understandably lost his patience. "Speak out, girl! What's the matter with you?"

"It — it was the doctor. He said how-the-Hell-do-you-get-this-damned-singlet-undone? And the dentist didn't know either so they got a pair of scissors and CUT MY NEW SINGLET RIGHT OFF ROUND THE NECK..."

They laughed, actually laughed, the pair of them. And it was my best singlet Mother had made for me, only the week before.

· · · · ·

XVI

Something will have to be done

"So this is where you are," Father said, and by his tone I knew at once I was in trouble. I couldn't think why he was wearing the familiar *what a trial it is to be a parent* look. My conscience was absolutely clear. I wasn't even hiding in the tall corn, I'd merely been spending a pleasant half hour plaiting into neat braids the luxurious, silky corn hair. Although the corn silk was only a few inches long it braided beautifully and looked neat and tidy tied at the ends with scraps of blue wool I'd retrieved from Granny's sewing basket.

At sight of all those growing green cobs pig-tailed like flaxen-haired little girls Father had to laugh. "What will you get up to next?" he said, and ruffled my own ginger locks. "A pity you don't take that much trouble with your fine head of hair."

Fine head of hair? Gosh, no one had ever said that to me before. Carrot-top, gingernut, rusty-nob, I'd heard them all, even Rufus the Red. But this was something else again. Perhaps it wasn't such a ghastly tragedy to have red hair after all? Some people might even think it was pretty, though I doubted that.

"Now listen to me," Father broke into my rose-coloured dreams of great beauty, "don't let me have to speak to you again about that stupid old hen of yours. If you can't keep the wretched creature inside the run where she belongs — well, something will have to be done about it, that's all."

I knew what that meant. Something had had to be done about our black spaniel puppy. He wouldn't stay tied up no matter how often we took him back to his kennel and fastened his collar around his neck again. The boys said it was because his neck was too fat, the collar slipped over the wrinkles and let him loose. I couldn't help wondering how Mr So-and-So kept his white collar in place over his wrinkles of fat, but the boys said I'd better not ask him. They said it wouldn't help to ask him, anyway, because his collar would come off over his head, too, if it had a chain on it and he was pulling back for all he was worth.

The puppy began at one end of Father's rows of broad beans and worked through and over and under them until there were none left standing. Not one. Another time he got into the cream. It would have been bad enough if he'd taken a drink out of the vat but he had to fall in.

We'd never seen a puppy encased in cream, not ever before. It was a frightening sight, a great animated blob of thick, rich cream, plus a couple of almost indistinguishable eyes and a wheezing, greasy bark.

Father had to throw out the whole consignment, though I think he was briefly tempted to send it to the dairy factory, anyway. Who was to know a puppy had taken its morning dip in the butter they were spreading on their toast?

The cream was not to be entirely a write-off, Father said. He fed it to the pigs that evening in place of their usual diet of skim milk. The result surprised and dismayed even the pigs; ten out of the mob of twenty-two died overnight. They couldn't accept such undreamed of luxury, such intemperance.

Granny said she'd heard of choking a cat with cream but to choke a pig with cream was just ridiculous. But then, what could one expect? Hanging was no lesson to some people. If she'd known what she knows now when a certain English aristocrat came courting her only daughter — farming, indeed! He didn't know one end of a piece of rope from another, and even to say that was praising him.

Something was very nearly done about the puppy at that time but after listening to me sniffling and bawling all evening Father weakened and said he'd give the dog — and us — one more chance. "Just one though, mind you," he warned.

The dog subsequently had his one more chance and blew it. Half a dozen dead hens on the back lawn in what looked like the results of a gigantic feather pillow fight was not an amusing sight. Even we children realised at last something would have to be done about

Bonzo the spaniel pup. We never saw him again. In a moment of rare gentleness Granny told us he'd gone to join the dear little puppies playing in the clouds up yonder, but we knew better. We'd come across a discreet but suspiciously new looking mound down by the creek, about the length and breadth of Bonzo...

And now something was going to have to be done about Speckly, my obstinate and inquisitive old hen. It seemed she had flown absent-mindedly in through the bedroom window and just as light-heartedly made herself a nest in the centre of Mother's hand-crocheted white lace bedspread.

It wasn't the egg Father was objecting to, it was the incredible amount of summer dust, and the feathers, and the threads pulled out of the delicate white lace by Speckly's scratchy old claws.

"Something will have to be done about that hen," Father repeated, "Upsetting your mother like this!"

Mother was not easily upset, she was calm and understanding and almost always saw the humorous side of anything that happened. I could imagine her mixed feelings, though, when she found the bedspread she'd brought from England all torn and dusty. Never mind the egg. We had plenty of eggs in more orthodox places round the farm.

I put Speckly under a box with water to drink and enough wheat to sink a ship. Every day I'd let her out to run around and scratch for worms and perhaps fly if she felt like stretching her wings. Then I'd shut her up again with a big stone on the box. She didn't have a hope of getting free unless I was there to watch her and make sure she kept well away from crocheted bedspreads and newly-sown seed plots and all.

Everything went according to plan for three weeks. I'd almost forgotten the horror of the something-will-have-to-be-done threat, when the dogs knocked the box over and let Speckly out. We didn't even hear her agitated squawkings as she half ran, half flew across the lawns with the big black dogs in hot pursuit.

In she went through the open window of the bedroom where she had been so comfortable on her last visit. But this time the dogs were right behind her. It was no trouble for those fence-jumping cattle dogs to clear the bedroom window sill.

Oh, brother! What an upset. Before anyone could get to the trouble spot Mother's crystal dressing-table set was scattered and parts of it smashed on the floor; the washstand basin plus the large matching jug of water tipped onto the bed; a curtain was ripped from its hangings...

"Something will have to be done about that hen." Never mind the dogs who started it all. Dogs will be dogs, I suppose, and anyway, they were too valuable, not like an old hen that didn't have the sense it was born with even.

Someone put her back under the box for the while and the dogs were chained up. I felt sick. It was awful about Mother's nice things getting broken and everyone was truly sorry, but chopping off Speckly's head wasn't going to mend anything.

When tea-time came round and everyone was in the dining room I slipped out and took her to the creek and threw her up into the air, hard. I think she thought I'd gone mad but at least she spread her gnarled old wings enough to carry her the rest of the way across the creek.

I couldn't see exactly where she landed. The banks of the creek were waist high in bracken fern and rushes and raupo, but she didn't try to come back so I felt comfortably certain she'd found a congenial new world for herself.

"You're late for your tea," Father rebuked me. "How many times do I have to tell you children not to keep your mother serving up your meals till all hours?"

Grown-ups can be unfair but I forgave the injustice this time. After all, he didn't know I'd just saved him the trouble of having to do something about old Speckly.

A couple of days later she was back, a bit ruffled and with a few more feathers than usual missing but as cheeky as ever. Father had taken it for granted she was dead, possibly by the hand of fate in the shape of cattle dogs. Not being sure whether her reappearance would be taken for granted — even Father's beliefs might not encompass a hen-ghost — I took her back to the creek.

This time she landed in full view on the opposite bank and took off noisily into the manuka and small shrubs. That was definitely the last time I ever set eyes upon old Speckly, but there was an

· · · · ·

interesting sequel. At school a few days later one of our Maori schoolmates told the story of a speckled old hen who had come knocking at their back door, so to speak.

She's a little beauty, he said, and they were going to keep her forever. That was good, Speckly's future was to be well taken care of, just as long as something didn't have to be done about her. I managed to seem casual and almost uninterested when I asked the boy if his mother had a white crocheted bedspread. The sun came out brightly for me when he said no, she didn't have one. So that was all right.

I missed the old hen. She'd let me dress her in dolls' clothes so long as she could still see out from under the bonnet, and she'd perch on my shoulder and let me take her anywhere I went on the farm. Anywhere except down the caves. She wouldn't go down there. I think she thought it was a rat-hole.

Things were more peaceful at home now she'd gone. There was nothing more for Father to have to do something about and I had almost forgotten the phrase with all its gloomy implications until Granny came out with it one day.

She was mopping up great muddy footprints off the kitchen floor. "Oh dear!" She shook her head. "Just look at this mud carried in on those gumboots! All I can say is this, SOMETHING WILL HAVE TO BE DONE ABOUT YOUR FATHER!"

XVII

Sunday afternoon walk

Flood waters were running high and turbulent in that part of the harbour known as the Narrows, so the visiting minister wasn't going to be able to get through to us in his small launch. He had been known to take hair-raising risks in his efforts to reach preaching places but no one could get far in a launch which was being swept back two yards for every one gained.

We youngsters were rather disappointed, the parson-cum-engine-driver was our favourite among the churchmen of various denominations who preached in our large front room. He was also a crack shot with the boys' air-gun and could beat us all at target practice.

We felt that Father would like to have objected to the gun being brought out on the Sabbath day but could not find the right words with which to rebuke so dedicated a young man of God. It was not as though we were aiming at live targets, our visitor would never have abetted us in any form of cruelty.

So here we were left with a whole long Sunday afternoon and nothing planned. After Bernard had been caught riding his horse up the steps and across the floor of the boys' outside bedroom, and the other boys were found in the act of staging a demonstration of tightrope walking on a thin wire stretching from ceiling-height to ceiling-height across the room, Father took over.

He'd take us younger ones for a long walk out to the back of the farm, a nice peaceful family Sunday afternoon walk.

The news was received in gloomy silence. We knew all about nice peaceful Sunday walks, we'd been caught that way before, many times. We did not enjoy being regimented into a neat little group and practically forced to accompany a grown-up for what seemed like hundreds of miles in the mid-summer heat.

We suspected Father didn't really enjoy the expedition any more than we did. He would undoubtedly have preferred to lounge comfortably in his armchair pretending to read the latest papers from home, but in fact taking a well-earned doze. One can't rise and shine at four o'clock every morning of the week without being overcome by drowsiness at unguarded moments.

This being so we considerately gave him every chance to sleep the afternoon away, but Granny had other ideas. "If you're going for a walk for Heaven's sake go, and take your brood with you."

We weren't exactly sure of the meaning of the word 'brood' but the way Granny came out with it there could be little doubt it was an insult. Father went off in a huff to change into heavier farm boots.

With touching solicitude we offered to stay home and keep Mother and Granny company. They might need us if, say, the cows broke down the gate and stampeded into the vegetable garden, or the pigs broke out of their run, or — well, anything could happen to a couple of defenceless women once our valiant young backs were turned. Visitors might arrive, for instance, and find no one at home to talk to, barring the same couple of women. The odds were too great against our going away from home that afternoon, surely Granny in her wisdom could see that?

But Granny remained unmoved. "You'd make good lawyers, the pack of you," was her only comment.

So when Father came back into the room we reacted rather hopelessly to the situation. Still, it was worth a few more tries. As he drank a hasty cup of tea we approached Father one at a time with excuses we thought believable, but all to no avail.

Father honestly meant the walk as a treat for us whereas we regarded the whole proceeding as a form of punishment. Very occasionally our boredom was relieved by some unrehearsed incident such as one of the boys falling into the creek and all the other boys diving in to rescue him. It didn't seem to matter that the boy in the water could swim like a fish and had slipped off the bridge intentionally, as they very well knew.

Poor Father, giving up his Sunday afternoon to a pack of young ingrates. Someone should have told him you can't turn a high-spirited mob of youngsters into a dove-cote of meekly fluttering birds of peace overnight. We must have driven him crazy, but punishment was out of the question as we always managed on these compulsory outings to keep within the letter of the law.

Shuffling along in the hot dust three or four lengths behind Father this Sunday we compared notes only to find we'd overplayed our hands when dealing out excuses. Four perfectly healthy young brats couldn't possibly all have developed raging earache within a few moments.

"What made you pick on earache?" Mack muttered, scowling. "You know I'm the one that gets earache. You're supposed to stick to toothache, you spoilsport."

I defended myself hotly. "Oh, yes? I suppose you do know I haven't got any bad teeth in my mouth? So how can I say they're aching?"

"I said my ears were aching and I haven't got any bad teeth in my ears, have I, nitwit?"

"They can't look in your ears and see they're not aching like they can teeth."

"Granny can," Mack said gloomily, "and she did. She said if my ears were aching so were her teeth."

"She's got take-out teeth!"

"Well? So what?"

The conversation was getting us nowhere, we still hadn't managed to pinpoint the person responsible for the collapse of our well-thought-out excuses. Ahead of us Father had paused and was regarding us with suspicion. "Can't you walk a little faster?"

"No," Edgar muttered, just a shade louder than he'd intended. Father came back to us.

"You'll keep up with me and enjoy our walk together," he said sternly, taking my hand and shepherding the boys in a shuffling group ahead of him. "Earache! When I was a lad I'd have been glad to have my father take me for a restful and enjoyable Sunday walk."

We got the picture. Poor little fellow deprived of the one great treat of any child's life, a Sunday walk with his father. We supposed his father was drunk. Granny had said the amount of champagne that man could drink was just nobody's business, so he probably would be too drunk to walk straight of a Sunday afternoon. I supposed it wouldn't hurt to ask Father if this was so.

· · · · ·

After that the Sunday outing really did become explosive. "You're trying to annoy me so that you'll be sent home," Father accused me. "If you children didn't want to come for a walk with me you only had to say so. You're here now, so stop making excuses and behaving like ignorant young savages."

Ignorant...? "I've just remembered," Mack brightened, "I was meant to be doing my homework this afternoon."

Father received this remarkable display of an awakening conscience coldly. "You can do your homework when we get back to the house."

"But we'll be milking the cows then..."

The cavalcade came to an abrupt stop. "One more excuse and I'll have to punish the lot of you," Father promised. "Now, are you fit to carry on or shall I have to bring a wheelchair for you?"

We carried on along the route of half-a-hundred similar excursions. Suddenly we were down off the Sahara-dry scoria ground and cooling our bare feet in the long, lush clover grass of the river flats.

Father stood, drinking in the mingled scents of purple pennyroyal flowers underfoot and heavy-headed cabbage-tree blooms overhead. A group of golden kowhai trees outlined their beauty against an impossibly blue summer sky. Nearby, scarlet kiekie berries hung festooned from silver-green leaf beds. And the larks! I have always loved to listen to the larks singing so high in the sky no one could possibly see them.

"Peaceful," Father breathed, "and so beautiful."

That was the trouble, the beauty of the whole scene was taking me by the throat. It was too utterly perfect, like when we all gathered round the wood fire on a winter's evening, the whole family, even the cats, and Mother read aloud to us, or played the piano, or we just sat and talked and no one squabbled.

"Beautiful," Father seemed unaware of secret mutterings and restless scuffling of bare feet. "Even in England you wouldn't find a scene as lovely as this."

Out of a full heart I wailed, "It makes my stomach ache. I want to go home to Mother."

That really put the cat among the pigeons. Our Sunday walk was off to a fresh start in heavy silence. The boys managed rather cleverly to drop back until the hindmost of them was chains away. It didn't work. They were marshalled back into line again and forced to continue along the happy path Father had mapped out for us.

We crossed the De Thierry creek and climbed the hill to see how the new grass was coming along. "Very good," Father pronounced, "A perfect take of Kentucky Blue Grass and a fair sprinkling of cocksfoot. There's no point in sowing paspalum on the hills, it makes a more satisfactory carpet for the river flats. Buffalo grass the same."

One of the boys had found a patch of tall yellow-flowered plants. "What's the name of this plant?"

"You know the name, son. Goodness me, that's a well known species of plant here in the North."

"But what is it called?"

"It's called rape, you know that. Why are you asking me?"

"I just wanted to be sure," my brother replied, "because I told the teacher that was what it was called and she wouldn't believe me. She said you should have more sense than to use words like that in our hearing."

I had to put my say in. "She didn't go mad at me when I told her the name of the lotus major grass growing round the school."

"Well, never mind about that," Father swept the whole subject under the carpet. Eyeing Edgar's contortions with a jaundiced eye he barked, "And might I ask what's the matter with you this time?"

"I've got a bee sting in my foot…"

"Ouch! Ow! So have I! Oooh, it hurts! I guess we'd better go home and put some washing blue on it…"

Father was not amused. He said, "Anyone else for the stings?" and he made the boys go and soak their feet in the cool waters of the nearby creek. I think he knew as well as any of us did there were no stings.

"Just tell me one thing," he eyed me sorrowfully, "why is it you children hate to come walking with me of a Sunday afternoon? You do hate it, all of you, don't you? And I try my best to make the walk interesting for you all."

He was waiting for my answer. I said, Heaven help me, "It's good fun, going for walks. The… the boys like it too."

• • • • •

They would probably have killed me if they'd overheard my blatant treachery. I felt pretty bad about the fibs I was telling, but what could I do when Father looked so hurt and disillusioned with us all? After all, he had given up a peaceful afternoon in the cool of the house with Mother.

"It's good fun," I said again, stoutly, and hoped God was not listening to my double-faced lies.

"Well, watch out for the bees," I swear there was a twinkle in Father's English-blue eyes. "We can't have you finding excuses to run for home."

We climbed to the top of the hill, looked down into the dense, untouched native forest on the other side beyond our boundary fence, then came hurrying away from the sound of wild horses screaming as they fought — a hideously terrifying sound. Even Father seemed glad to find himself back on the other side of the creek.

The atmosphere had become more relaxed, more cordial, with the sharing of a common fear. Those horses could have attacked us if they'd known of our presence and could have got at us through the boundary fence.

Still, we were all safe and there was no longer the necessity to dream up excuses, we were on our way home in any case. So Father must have been puzzled when he caught up with us as we scampered ahead of him across the scoria rocks only to find me yelling blue murder and with my big toe generously swathed in the frill torn from my white lace petticoat.

"I want to go home," I wailed, "My foot's sore!"

"Not you too, Nora," Father looked sad. "What is the excuse this time, another bee sting? Let me have a look at that toe..."

"Don't touch it — it's sore!" Both my hands were clasped round the swathed bandages. "I just want to go home!"

"No doubt," said Father dryly. "Well, get up and go home then, you silly child. Unless you can't walk on that wounded toe of yours?"

"We'll carry her," the boys offered. "She's a skinny little rat anyway. We can easily carry her between the lot of us."

While Father stared at them in obvious astonishment at the lengths to which they were prepared to take the pretence I sat myself down on the nearest rock and watched, fascinated, the great spurt of blood soaking through the bindings.

"It's the whole toe-nail," Mack explained. "She kicked the nail clean off at the roots. We were racing each other, we didn't see the rock in the path..."

XVIII

Mop

Quite early on, Father decided the saying *Handsome is as handsome does* did not apply to the cattle dog, Mop. The black-and-white collie was certainly extraordinarily handsome but as a cattle dog he was proving himself useless. He was intelligent enough, goodness knows — too intelligent! He'd worked out in his canine mind just why he was in this world — he'd been placed here to have a darned good time and that was exactly what he meant to do with his life.

Send him out into the paddocks to round up the cows and bring them to the milking sheds and he'd rush off earnestly enough, but bring in the cows? Don't be stupid! On a beautiful day like this, with rabbits to be chased and a hundred intriguing rustlings and cheepings going on in the long grass? The cows could look after themselves, who cared if they were an hour late getting to the sheds?

As for driving sheep, it just wasn't on. His sympathies were all with the wool-laden, hot and panting mob he was supposed to be hurrying along the road. If they wanted to nibble the dusty grass of the road verges or even push through under roadside fences and scamper across other farmers' meadows that was okay by him. He had a flair for that sort of thing himself.

He'd once even gone to no end of trouble to lead a mob of sheep down a side road to a cool, rippling creek he knew of. Never mind the shouting and yelling and whistling that was going on behind him. The farmers were entitled to their own peculiar forms of entertainment and if they wished to shout and whistle — well, why not? Personally, he preferred a long cool drink at the creek and so, it would seem, did the sheep. It was just a pity they'd had to go two miles out of their way to find the creek.

Still, why worry? If they were late for today's sheep sale there'd be another tomorrow. Life was too short to rush hysterically here and there like humans seemed to do.

The people who gave Mop to Father were quite frank about their reasons for getting rid of so handsome and obviously intelligent an animal. He was Hell on a farm, they said, but Father was known to be pretty good with animals and if he thought he could do anything with this canine playboy he was welcome to try.

The swap should have worked well. Father was indeed good with animals, no doubt because of his understanding and affection for them. So why should the strongest possible antipathy develop almost immediately between him and the newcomer?

Mop took one look into Father's neatly bearded countenance and slunk behind me, his tail between his legs. If this was an English aristocrat he, Mop, was having nothing to do with the breed. Come to think of it, he himself was an aristocrat among collies, he was registered and had a lengthy pedigree to prove his claim. So who did this new owner think he was, anyway?

As for Father, his snort of derision when he set eyes upon the dog spoke for itself. Mop was too handsome. A dog as handsome as that was bound to be as useless and irritating as a too-handsome man. Still, he'd try Mop out and if he proved his worth he'd keep him. A man couldn't be fairer than that, he said, but just let that... Adonis start worrying the hens or any nonsense like that and he'd go pretty smartly.

We hadn't known Father was so fond of the hens; squawking, flighty creatures that he named them. I caressed Mop's shining black head, brushed down with my hands his snow-white ruff and silently vowed I'd do anything — I'd sleep out in the hen run if that would avoid trouble between the hens and Mop. Between Father and Mop.

Father was as good as his word. He gave Mop every chance to become an asset to the farm. It was a waste of time. Mop was not turning over a new leaf just to please someone he didn't like much anyway. In spite of the established rule, one dog, one master, the boys were allowed to try their hand at training the newcomer, but Mop treated their efforts as part of the joke.

No one was laughing when he came back from a game of seven-a-side with a neighbour's young turkeys. The neighbour had intended to kill them for Christmas Day, but this was only August. I despaired for Mop's future. How could he be taught that what was sauce for the dog was not — was definitely not sauce for the turkeys? Romping round a ten-acre paddock was fun for him but a little too strenuous for his feathered friends. No one had ever told him turkeys are not by nature energetic birds.

To keep the peace Father had to buy the victims. Since he didn't like turkey meat in the first place and certainly could never look a turkey in the face after a prolonged diet of roast turkey hot, roast turkey cold, roast turkey in the pot nine days old, relations between himself and his dog were not the best.

Even the boys were losing their patience with Mop. A joke is a joke, they appreciated a bit of fun as much as the next one, but saddles were much too expensive even in those days to be chewed to pieces. Bridles, too, went mysteriously missing. As Bernard said, it wouldn't be so maddening if the dog meant to make use of the purloined articles himself, but who ever saw a great oaf of a black-and-white collie perched astride a galloping mount? It was much better fun putting the horses through their paces in a wild sprint round the paddocks, urged on by the occasional sharp nip to their flying heels.

The bell tolled for Mop when one of Father's best young cows came gambolling from the back of the farm, taking fences and all in her stride. Her roars of anguish could be heard even before we spotted her ballet-dance approach. She seemed uncertain whether to progress backwards, in circles, or by means of an elegant roll towards us over the short-cropped grass. She did in fact try out all three methods.

From my vantage point up the nearest tree I saw the poor thing's tail was bleeding at the tip. Father and the boys had made the same discovery and were trying to catch her and calm her down. The brush of her tail was missing and so was a two-inch portion of the tail itself.

"She's caught her tail in the barbed wire fence," Father pronounced, rendering first aid while the boys clung to the animal's neck to keep her captive. "I never have approved of barbed wire, but what can one do? Plain wire is useless against the attacks of the wilder run cattle."

I'd condescended by now to come down from my exalted perch

and join the others. We could all see how upset Father was by the animal's suffering, though some of the boys were cynical about the tragedy. Lots of cows lost the ends of their tails and took no notice. Farmers even cut the end off, especially when any cow developed the habit of switching them in the face with a bunch of wire-strong muddy hair when milking was in progress.

"Never mind about what other farmers do," Father said crisply, "How do you suppose I can put this young pedigree cow in the Jersey cattle show now her looks have been ruined?"

"If you could find her tail you could sew it on again," Edgar suggested in all seriousness. His enthusiasm must have been a bit dashed by the look Father gave him. He added hastily, "I don't suppose you could find it, anyway."

The cow had been restored to a degree of calmness and we were leaving the scene when Mop supplied the answer Edgar was seeking. With the air of a foxhound returning with the prized brush he laid the missing tail at my feet.

It was obvious the barbed wire had not been to blame. In one of his moments of light-hearted abandon Mop had bitten off the tail. His strong tusks would make nothing of the job.

After that his fate was sealed. In spite of the fact that I kept a sharp eye on him for the next few days I missed out on the final scene. Father knew I would hear the shot if he chose that way to get rid of Mop so, against his humanitarian impulses I should hope, he decided to quietly drown the big dog. It was to be a clandestine deed in the dark of the night. Kittens, not yet old enough to sense what was happening to them, had been disposed of in this way. We accepted that, even though we hated the necessity to keep down the count of our dozen or so cats.

But Mop! He was my good mate. I probably loved him more than I did my own brothers. And he loved me, too. When the men were firing off great blasts of dynamite to make a new roadway Mop had learned to recognise their warning yells before the blast. It was the signal for him to rush into the house and hide behind me. No one else had ever trusted me to that gratifying extent.

There was a commotion on the back verandah at about two in the morning. Most of us woke up and rushed out to see what was going on. By the light of our electric torches we spotted Mop cowering in a corner, whimpering and absolutely sopping wet. Even as we discovered his presence he shook himself vigorously all over us, muddy river water, scraps of weed and all.

If Mop was adding midnight fishing excursions to his many and varied hobbies I'd never be able to keep an eye on him. I was trying to dry his coat with an old towel when we heard someone stumbling up the path in the dark. We couldn't believe our eyes — it was Father, and he was as wet and dejected-looking as Mop. In our astonishment we almost expected him to shake muddy river water over us, too.

"Where's that dog?" He must have been blinded not to spot Mop cringing there. "Out of the way, girl." He pushed my protective arms aside and grabbed Mop by the collar. By now Mother had joined us on the porch and it was she who protested.

"Oh, no, Norman! Not in front of the children!"

"What are you talking about?" Father was glaring at her for probably the first time ever. "Get the dog that steak out of the meat safe," he ordered me, "and take him in by the stove to get warm. Come on, now! What are you all staring at?"

As ever, I began to cry. Father must be positively dangerous — who ever heard of anything so terrible as drying out a dog before the fire and feeding him on juicy steaks when he was meant to be drowned again at once?

We children never did hear the full story but we picked up enough to know that Father had accidentally fallen into the river from a slippery bank in the pitch dark. Mop was there in the water first of course, but somehow he'd had the intelligence to free himself from the heavy stone tied to his neck.

Just as well, or Father would have drowned too. It was Mop who lent his powerful strength in helping Father to the shore. No wonder he was being fed tomorrow's steak dinner. There was no more talk of getting rid of him, though I feel sure Father came mighty close, more than once, to forgetting the saving grace of human gratitude.

When, for instance, Mop developed a habit of thumping his tail against the glass doors at the front of the house. In the middle of the night this unfamiliar thump, thump had us all guessing. We thought it might be Mop but if so he managed to vanish into thin air before any of us could get to the door to check on his activities.

Opening the door to nothingness was quite unnerving. Father was the only one who found an excitingly satisfying explanation. The rest of us steadfastly refused to believe in the supernatural.

We were too quick for the young monkey one night; his shadowy form was just disappearing round the corner of the house as we opened the door. Father would have preferred to go on believing it was not Mop at all. I think his bitterness stemmed from the conviction that even the family dog was tricking him and throwing ridicule over his beliefs.

Anyway, we left for Auckland shortly after that and I was allowed, incredibly, to take Mop with me. I guess Father was not game to drown him again and we couldn't leave him at the farm as the incoming family had half a dozen dogs of their own.

I don't think Mop liked suburban life much. He hung around me as though I was his only hope in a terrifying universe, which was all very well and highly flattering — but I did wish he wouldn't keep on gnawing through his rope leash and turning up in the classroom.

The school was more than a mile away and I was terrified he'd get himself collected en route. How he ever found me Heaven only knows. I'd never shown him round the classroom or even hinted where the school might be located.

After a while the head teacher who took our class tired of sending me home with the dog and became suspicious of my methods of restraining Mop. Did I tie him securely? Was I certain I'd shut him carefully in the new kennel? Had I by any chance arranged for neighbouring children to let him off or even take him for a run on the leash he was invariably dragging behind him?

I hadn't and I didn't, but all the same a heavy guilt persisted. I didn't want to dodge school anyway. I loved school and I liked the teacher very much, but nothing we tried kept Mop at home.

Chained to his kennel, he'd drag it round the yard till the chain snapped or the staples came out, leaving him free to sprint for the school. I shut him in the coal shed but that wasn't a smart move. He turned up in the classroom coated in coal dust and in his joy at seeing me still there apparently waiting for him he shook himself jubilantly all over everyone. The teacher wasn't pleased about that, either.

So once again amidst the discreet sniggering of the forty-odd classmates I grabbed him and ran him home through the streets, only to find everyone was out and there wasn't one safe spot to confine him to. He'd dug himself a sort of miniature London Underground system under the walls of the coalshed, his kennel was lying on its side, the leash broken, and over by the far garden hedge he'd excavated a bomb crater large enough to bury an army in. I guess his original intention had been to burrow under the hedge to the street beyond, but prickly holly isn't the hedge with which to conduct a comfortable and friendly argument.

I had no other course than to shove him into the laundry and lock the door on him. If he got out of there he'd put Houdini himself to shame.

Back in the classroom I sneaked into my desk and buried my red face in the English grammar book the others were studying, but it seemed I was not to be let off so lightly this time. While the class sat up as one and stared, goggle-eyed, I was called out to the front and told to stand by the teacher's table.

The teacher was smiling but I didn't trust anyone's smiles where Mop's antics were concerned. I was about to get the strap for the first time in my life, that was for sure. I decided I'd begin blubbing right away as I'd be bound to start off crying when the strap tore into my unaccustomed palm. The boys said it hurt like billy-oh when they got it.

"Take a look at her, children," the teacher said, placing a hand on my shrinking shoulder. Unfortunately I didn't at that time know the word 'sadist' or I might have found a measure of comfort in applying it silently to him.

Then he said, incredibly, ridiculously, "You are looking at a girl who has distinguished herself and her school by gaining one hundred marks out of a possible one hundred in essay composition. Now, what do you think of that, Nora?"

They were all staring at me and waiting but my mind was on much more important matters. I opened my mouth and wailed, "Please, sir, it isn't my fault…"

XIX

Festive occasion

Today was to be a holiday. We'd known about it for more than a week. The cows had to be milked, of course, and calves given their thrice-daily ration of skimmed milk and shark oil, but apart from these chores nothing was to be done on the farm. Not a tap of work between the lot of us.

At breakfast there was an air of subdued excitement. I think we shared a pessimistic fear that Father might change his mind and thrust our unwilling noses back against the proverbial grindstone if we kicked up too much of a din. We even went so far as to nudge neighbouring shins beneath the table and nod silently towards the marmalade or the toast rack as though a simple spoken request might start the tide of good fortune turning against us.

Holidays were rare indeed, Father having fallen between two stools, so to speak. He'd cut himself adrift from festive occasions in his homeland yet failed to develop any great interest in local red-letter days. Still, this was one day in the year we did get a real break.

The whole scene could not have been more perfect, and that included the weather. Father startled us by humming tunelessly as he meticulously combed his pointed beard and military-looking moustache in front of the bathroom mirror.

When he and Mother came out from England he'd boasted long flowing moustachios carefully waxed at the tips. Very impressive and a great asset to his looks but nevertheless they had to go. Only an idiot, Granny pronounced, would get his moustache so entangled in the armful of puriri fence posts he was carrying as to almost snap his neck in two when he threw the posts to the ground. The unpleasant shock must have literally brought him humbly to his knees.

It was Granny who threw cold water over our excitement this lovely spring holiday morning. It might be a holiday for some people but not for others, she hinted darkly. There were people in this house who had better things to do than dress up in their second-best clothes and sit about the house all day twiddling their thumbs and pretending not to know there was butter to churn and bread to be kneaded and put in the oven.

Never mind the fact that Wednesday was not baking nor butter-making day, all that had been done the day before. Granny could be surprisingly forgetful for so keen-witted an old lady. Still, she had Father looking uncomfortable and seeking for excuses which was after all the probable object of the whole exercise.

She drove the point home relentlessly. If certain persons whom she would not be unkind enough to mention by name would bestir themselves and go chop some firewood, or get up onto the roof and put a nail — just one nail, mind you — in that loose flapping piece of roofing iron, or fix the hinge on the hen-house door and while he was about it put in another row of nesting-boxes for the poor feathered creatures who had to wait their turn when it came time to lay their eggs of an early morning…

Don't talk such nonsense, Father erupted angrily. Perhaps she would like him to set to work and build a whole new hen-house before breakfast? A stupid fuss about nothing, that's all. The hens were perfectly satisfied and happy with the amount of nesting room they had.

"It's easy to talk," Granny clattered the spoons and forks she was washing. "You're not a hen."

"Is that so? Well, just excuse me for daring to stay alive, will you?" Father stalked out of the kitchen.

We youngsters were fond of Granny but there were times when our affection faltered. Did she really have to choose this moment to upset Father and endanger our holiday? But there was even worse to come.

"Like father, like children," she said. "I suppose you're all going to sit round the house all day, too, the whole brood of you?"

We thought this over. When Granny called us a 'brood' we knew she was, to put it in her own words, sick to death of having us under her feet the whole livelong day. I think it was Mack who came up with a brilliant suggestion.

"We could take our lunch up the De Thierry creek and thresh out the cocksfoot seed for Father?"

"A lot of grass seed you'd be threshing, my lad. You wouldn't even get as far as spreading the tarpaulins on the ground, much less cutting the dry seedheads and threshing them."

Granny was speaking rather more loudly than usual. It flashed into my mind she wanted Father to overhear what she was saying. "Besides," her voice rose to an even higher note, "it's no good talking about having a picnic day, your father wouldn't allow it."

"Who said I wouldn't allow it?" Father reappeared in the doorway, his tell-tale barometer of a moustache bristling angrily. "Who says I wouldn't allow my own children to go off and enjoy their holiday?"

After a moment he added, "In fact, I'll go with them and so will their mother."

So it was settled as Granny well knew it would be. Her psychological approach had been foolproof. We found ourselves on our way up the narrow creek which led to an old apple orchard at the back of the farm. We didn't doubt Granny's ability to console

Not the cream launch, but a Hokianga family picnic all the same

herself for the lack of our company. If she'd really wanted to be with us she could have come along too.

We had meant to row ourselves to the appointed spot but it was rather more fun putt-putting along in Father's launch. We took up almost the whole width of the waterway so that bank-side flax bushes swept the hull as we scraped through. Overhead willows drooped their wet branches to slosh us in the face as we chugged along beneath them. Anyone stupid enough to sit on top of the cabin would have been scraped off like a surplus quarter-pound of butter and flung ignominiously into the muddy creek.

As it was we created our own excitement by leaning over the side of the launch to wet our sun-scorched faces and heads in the wash from the bow, a circus-like performance which would have horrified Mother if she had chanced to glance out from the cool haven of the cabin. The fact that we held each other by the heels, taking turns at it, was no insurance. It would have been rather fun to let go and see what happened.

There was only one thing worrying us — how were we going to keep the grown-ups entertained all day? The old orchard was essentially a children's playground. Neither Mother nor Father would be interested in scaling the gnarled, scaly-barked, monkey-puzzle apple trees and even if they did wish to do a bit of tree-climbing the slim young manukas would hardly bear their weight.

No doubt Father would give us a hand with the grass seed project but we could not by the wildest stretch of the imagination picture Mother mowing with a sickle or threshing the dry grass-heads to extract the seeds.

"She might like to get hold of an axe and help Father chop out some of the ti-trees?" Edgar suggested. "Or bash out the dock plants Father is always going to market about? You know he hates the sight of dock coming up everywhere in the orchard."

We howled him down. His suggestion bordered on the blasphemous. Mother and a great, greasy, bludgeoning, insensitive axe or spade simply did not go together. Something would definitely have been lost if she'd begun thrashing and banging her way through life.

I wished Father wouldn't get such a set on every plant of dock he discovered on the farm. With five hundred acres to play around with you'd think he wouldn't begrudge a tiny bit of space to the docks. In my eyes the brilliant green and scarlet dock seeds were beautiful. I loved to run my fingers up the wiry seed stalk and strip off a handful of soul-satisfying colour.

As Edgar had said, Father hated the plant and was death and destruction to the whole species, especially the seedheads which he claimed spread docks willy-nilly over the whole countryside. So what? They weren't, as far as I could see, doing any harm. Stinging nettle, now, that was different — there was nothing beautiful about stinging nettles, they were mean, sneaky, vicious plants deliberately hiding in the long grass ready to grab you and poison your bare feet.

"If Father's going to chop out the dock I'm going home," I threatened, and meant it. Cocksfoot grass, yes. The seeds were sharp and barbed so that it was painful indeed if one flew into our eyes as we threshed the dry heads.

Father could do what he liked with the cocksfoot just as long as he left my friends the dock seeds alone. I supposed I was slightly disloyal, hating his very shadow when he went back to the orchard later and fetched his sickle from the launch. Dock heads, leaves and roots flew everywhere under the strength of his attack. I watched the awful carnage in sulky silence and refused to tell anyone why I was sullenly refusing to eat my share of the delicious lunch.

"It's easy to talk," Granny had retorted earlier that morning, "You're not a hen." Well, he wasn't a dock plant either, so there was nothing I could do about it. I could only vent my wounded feelings by filling both my pockets to overflowing with the discarded dock seeds.

Out of a blue sky the rain suddenly came pelting down, as it does in the far north. We covered the grass seed with waterproof tarpaulins and ran for the shelter of the launch. Granny would not welcome our early return but we couldn't help that. It would have been stupid to stay out in the rain all day just to get ourselves out from under her feet, so to speak.

As it happened her bark turned out to be worse than her bite, as was so often the case. We arrived home to find she'd started preparations for a five-star dinner that evening, complete with fruit salad and cream and nuts. We youngsters watched, goggle-eyed, until she turned on us and ordered us out of the kitchen.

"Go and get your presents ready, all of you. And see you write on the parcels this year so that your mother will know who they're from."

The boys scampered off but I stood there, petrified. I knew Father always took this day-long holiday in honour of Mother's birthday — I KNEW IT WAS HER BIRTHDAY AND I'D FORGOTTEN TO MAKE THE PINCUSHION FOR HER. I was too shocked even to cry.

"Well? Run along." Granny gave me a tiny shove with the back of her floury hand. "Get your present ready-wrapped before your father comes looking for it. He's likely to give you the rough edge of his tongue, tired and all as he is with chopping out that pestilent noxious weed. Run along, child!"

I went unwillingly, dragging my feet, but in a moment, happiness flooded over me in a great wave of relief. I didn't need to have made the pincushion, I'd thought of something a hundred times more interesting, more eye-catching. When Father opened my parcel along with all the others that evening he'd be able to put into Mother's hands a glass preserving jar full of the biggest, brightest and most beautiful of my cherished hoard of dock seeds.

Boating, possibly near Horeke, circa 1910.
ALEXANDER TURNBULL LIBRARY

XX

Beyond our ken

Our house was bathed in gloom. Mother seemed very quiet and not nearly as brightly humorous as usual. As for Father, he was really snappy. We younger children could do nothing right in his eyes.

The changed atmosphere puzzled me. I was much too young to realise the implications of the war being waged overseas, too young to grasp that our eldest brother was about to leave for the battlefront. To us youngsters it was a great lark having him home in a smart khaki uniform complete with tall lemon-squeezer hat and woollen puttees neatly patterning his calves from knee to ankle.

Our family had rather strangely divided itself into two groups: the five elder members, and the tight little band we four youngest had formed through the years. To us the elders were classed as grown-ups and as such were not entitled to membership within our younger ranks. All the same, we regarded them all with affection and respect. Anything our eldest brother in particular had to say carried great weight with us.

There was a dance at our place while he was home and everyone made a great fuss of him and said things like "have fun over there" and "see you when you come back, old chap." So we kids knew he was going off again somewhere and this was a farewell evening for him. I think we felt aggrieved that he should be allowed to take another long holiday away from the farm while we carried on in the same old groove, the occasional trip to Rawene in Father's launch our only excitement.

Still, he must have felt guilty about his good fortune. Otherwise, why should he suddenly decide to give his belongings away to us envious little stay-at-homes? His *Boys' Own Annuals*, his highly prized Maori adze, his leather whip and Mexican saddle, even his horse and dog — almost everything he owned was shared between us. Our mercenary instincts were lulled to rest. Let him have his holiday, by all means. We wished him every happiness during his absence.

A blazing row had blown up in the family months earlier. It seemed someone had posted Harold the white feather of cowardice, not realising in their patriotic fervour he was at that time too young to offer himself for active service in the army. He'd said nothing about this to any of us and especially not to Mother and Father. Why hurt their feelings by recording the insulting actions of an obvious fanatic? In any case he wasn't by any means the only recipient of the white feather; women who should have known better busied themselves mightily posting the emblem to any man who even looked to be of military age.

The quarrel began when Father happened to discover the feather and in righteous indignation pinned it to a photo of Harold in full dress uniform and posted it to the person who had sent it in the first place.

Okay. It was fair enough and wouldn't have caused more than a ripple in the family — if Father had chosen the right person to send it to. As it happened the recipient of his postal attentions had never sent a white feather to anyone in her life and wouldn't dream of doing so.

I don't know how he came to make such a mistake but this I do know, we lost a good friend of the family and Father was in the doghouse for days over it, especially as one of the elder boys had been lining up this same woman as a possible mother-in-law. Collapse of a promising young romance.

If I remember rightly final leave was in those days a period of three weeks. During most of that time our parents couldn't do enough for Harold, mother building up for his physical comfort a great barrier of knitted woollen socks and balaclavas and what-have-you, to say nothing of tins of home-made biscuits, cakes and goodies sufficient to sink a troopship.

Father confined his protective advice to the spiritual realm. No son of his was going to be allowed to stray from the straight and narrow path, no sir! Never mind the fact that the lad had already spent months in the sophisticated atmosphere of Trentham Army

Training camp and so was well aware of the possible pitfalls Father was delicately hinting at. His hilarious description of a first encounter with the effects of a mild-looking peppermint-flavoured drink called absinthe reduced us to helpless tears of mirth but was definitely not for Father's ears.

On the lighter side we organised lantern-slide evenings, euchre parties, moonlight picnics and daylight outings. The daddy of them all was the jaunt down-river on a three-hour trip to the Heads. We'd been on these trips before in Father's launch, leaving home about seven in the morning or earlier and returning late in the evening, painfully sunburned from the glare of semi-tropical sun on the desert-dry sandhills where we'd spent the day.

We could have sat out in the launch fishing for snapper or kahawai but we youngsters preferred to climb the mountain-high range of loose, wind-blown sand. We always hoped to make our way out to the open sea on the other coast but it was a wild ambition; the sand dunes stretched away as far as we could see.

Coming back to the picnic grounds was fun as long as one managed to keep from pitching forward down the mountain, taking the choice of cartwheeling end-over-end all the way down or digging in head first, ostrich-like, in the loose, incredibly hot sand.

True to my habitually pessimistic and cowardly nature I found my day clouded by gloomy anticipation. When it came time to go home we would have to clamber precariously up onto the tall bow of Father's launch, or if the sea was too rough for him to bring the launch in close enough we'd find ourselves loaded a few at a time into a small, rickety dinghy and ferried out across white-tipped waves to the restless, tossing craft.

I suppose it wasn't so very craven of me to dread the ordeal. After all, even Mother seemed white-faced and shaken by the time we were all gathered together in the comforting safety of the sturdy launch. The boys, of course, loved every moment of it, the rougher the better.

Another day we went with Harold on his favourite walk through almost trackless native bush to the comparatively clear area which had once been a church mission station. Bricks from the chimney were still there after all those generations had come and gone. A moss-grown orchard still boasted a few mandarins, plums, pears and mulberries. We walked through a sea of arum lilies and jonquils, with maidenhair ferns flourishing in the shelter of encroaching gorse.

And of course nearby was the huge, spreading, quite famous Waima oak tree, one of the largest in the Southern Hemisphere, we were told at school. We swam in the creek then ate our picnic lunch perched like monkeys among its rustling leaves.

A half-mile or so away we could hear the Maori people singing beautifully. Wedding festivities were in progress which would last a week or more. We'd spotted whole carcasses hanging in the trees: pigs, cattle and sheep. It was to be quite some hangi, a spectacular feast. Too bad we had missed out on an invitation to this one.

Dinner at home that evening was a quiet affair. Even we exuberant young brats sensed that our chatter was not in keeping with the general atmosphere. We wondered what all the fuss was about. It was after all Harold's own choice to leave us tomorrow. He didn't have to go off on another holiday so soon if he didn't wish to.

After dinner we sat round the table listening to the grown-ups' sketchy conversation. Mother was quiet and seemed to be urgently taken up with her little game of making tiny heaps of breadcrumbs on the white tablecloth then as carefully sweeping them away again.

Harold was quiet, too, but suddenly he startled us all. He'd got to his feet and was standing there with his eyes closed. After a moment he began to talk to Mother but none of us knew what he was saying. He was speaking quickly in a language none of us had ever heard before — and neither had he.

It was quite frightening. He didn't even look like himself but seemed older and much more… definite, sort of. He spoke for, I suppose, about a minute, almost a harangue, then he smiled and in broken English told Mother not to worry, her son would return to his family safe and sound.

Harold opened his eyes and wouldn't believe them when they told him what had taken place. I don't think he ever did quite believe it happened, he thought he'd merely dozed off for a moment.

XXI
Friends and neighbours

Someone once said to me, "You must surely have had an unusual childhood up there in the Hokianga, so terribly isolated. No neighbours, no friends, no visitors. How ghastly!"

I don't know where she picked up her weird ideas, her distorted picture of the North. We had neighbours, close Maori neighbours who were also our good friends. Our Pakeha friends were equally compatible and loyal. We enjoyed their company as often as pressure of farm work and other circumstances would permit.

As for visitors, we had many from Auckland and points further south who thoroughly enjoyed riding round the farm, rowing on the river, fishing and picnicking thirty miles away at the mouth of the harbour where Father had taken them in his launch. And of course everyone enjoyed Mother's fabulous farm meals.

I have to admit we were isolated during the winter months by scary river floods, our whole farm becoming a sea of debris-strewn, swirling, muddy waters. Well, not quite the whole farm, there were higher-level areas where the animals sought or were guided to safety, and the house was set high on a volcanic rise which had at one time been used as a Maori pa, a sort of stockade.

The rising flood seldom caught Father unawares but I do remember after a sudden cloudburst seeing every skerrick of the top-grade, heart kauri sawn timber so dear to Father's heart swept from its storage shed and carried off on the torrent, shed and all.

The timber was meant to have been used in the building of a new house. The guest room was to have been quite something, but personally I could see nothing wrong with the guest room we already had. Except that a guest room of any type involved me in extra duties. I never did enjoy housework and resented the boring responsibility of keeping the guest room wash-hand basin and jug spotless and filled with fresh water the whole time visitors were with us.

Mother would have considered it poor hospitality not to have wiped down the marble-topped washstand and burnished the carafe with its matching crystal tumbler at least twice every day.

I still can't for the life of me see why visitors couldn't come to the kitchen tap for a drink of water when thirst gripped them. I don't recall anyone ever drinking the water from the carafe, anyway. They no doubt preferred a cup of tea or coffee.

The hospitable custom of that time was to place two big soft white towels and two coloured ones in the room, plus a covered glass dish of sweets and a selection of reading matter. The guest's favourite soap, too. Few of our guests smoked, certainly none of the women, so there was no problem of choosing the favourite brand of cigarettes, but for more favoured visitors there was a tiny bottle of their chosen scent. If visitors didn't feel welcome on that backblocks farm it certainly wasn't Mother's fault.

Unfortunately there were the inevitable few guests who moved in indefinitely and were insensitive that even the most generous hospitality can wear thin after prolonged strain. Especially when five-star hotel attention was not only taken for granted but was fully expected every day of the week.

When broad hints and even outspoken requests failed to shift a guest who had been under our roof for five long weeks and seemed to have taken root for life, some bright member of the family came up with a scheme to dislodge him. It seemed an awfully good scheme but not perhaps for parental consideration.

We youngsters began seeing our share of Father's ghosts. A warning shriek would bring our dilatory guest to his feet. "Don't sit in that chair! Grandfather's sitting there — you'll squash him flat if you sit on him!"

Since it was well known both our grandfathers were long gone from this world of sorrows we were vaguely surprised by the effect of our warning. Our guest had always maintained he didn't believe in spirit manifestations. He'd been almost insulting to Father over the question of resident ghosts here on the farm. And here he was leaping practically out of the window at the merest hint that someone had moved into his chair ahead of him.

The unexpected success went to our heads. We developed

clairvoyance to the highest degree, and since we had no wish to selfishly keep our new-found ESP gift to ourselves, we shared every experience with our friend. Unlike us, he didn't enjoy the awareness that there were others beside us humans inhabiting this sphere. He even developed a habit of asking us if it was all right to sit down here or there, or was the seat occupied by Great-Aunt Hilda, or Uncle James, or someone he hadn't even heard of?

He began to shun bedtime and seemed grateful when one or other of the boys inspected his bed to make sure Big Bear wasn't already there, sound asleep. We should all have been shot. It's really a wonder we weren't the object of some demented victim's just wrath.

This obtuse young man put up with our blackmailing attacks for longer than might have been expected, though he was definitely showing the strain. He jumped at every shadow, but his appetite seemed quite unaffected. All the same, we'd hear him tossing and turning in his room most of the night. The boys reported that he was keeping his kerosene wall-lamp burning all night, which from our inhuman angle was a good sign. Surely it wouldn't be long now till he vacated our spare room.

He'd retired with marked reluctance to his room one dark and weirdly stormy evening when those of us still in the living room were startled by his abrupt reappearance. His pale eyes were starting out of the folds of fat creased around them. His loose, full lips hung open in abject terror.

From the little sense we could get out of him we learned there was a full-sized ghost in his room. It was a man, not young, dressed in a plus-four golfing suit. The ghost had not spoken to him, it merely stood there, staring, its smile far from friendly.

Father was the only one of us quite unmoved. He seemed delighted that so blatant an unbeliever had been brought summarily to heel. We could see that he never for one moment doubted the authenticity of the vision. But then Father had not been told of the sudden influx of ethereal beings to our humble farmhouse.

Actually, I think I was a bit angry and fed up with the whole scheme. Giving the guest a few good frights was all right and only what anyone so thick-skinned deserved, but there could be danger in scaring the life out of him.

After the trembling victim had been persuaded to go to his room again I went in search of my reprobate young brothers. "You could have been in trouble…" I began, but they were staring incredulously.

"We weren't anywhere near his room! We thought it was you dressed up."

"Of course it was me, I always go round dressed in plus four golf clothes," I withered them with my sarcasm. How stupid could the boys become! It couldn't have been anyone but them.

Even poor Father had been deceived. He'd said the apparition was undoubtedly his grandfather. The description was exact in every detail, he said, even to the unsmiling face for which his grandfather was well known. Also, his grandfather was a great fan of golf and practically always wore plus fours.

I stormed at the boys, "It's bad enough playing tricks on the visitor but now you've gone and dragged Father into it. If he finds out you kids have been having him on…"

"Stop fooling and tell us where you found the plus fours," Mack was beginning to lose his temper. "A joke is a joke but you can cut it out now and tell us how you worked the trick."

"I didn't work any trick!" The truth was slowly seeping through to all of us. There were no golf clothes in the house. None of us could possibly have dressed up in non-existent clothes. So? And anyway, how could we look like Father's grandfather, frowning face and all?

"But he really saw… someone…"

"He was scared to death…"

I began to back tremblingly out of the boys' room but was halted by an urgent request. "Don't put the light out, nitwit! If you think we're going to get off to sleep in the dark…!"

Mother imported from the city a young girl of my own age as company for me but I'm afraid Mother's kindly gesture was not appreciated by either of us. Our guest undertook to put me through a pressurised ladies' finishing school course. Until she pointed them out I had never given a thought to the freckles spattering my nose.

Nor had I even in my most imaginative moments ever thought of my unruly ginger locks as 'gorgeously auburn kiss-curls.' I said, "Help! Excuse me while I be sick," and she retorted, "I was only trying to be kind. Your hair is actually a terrible mess, like mashed carrots without any salt."

What the salt had to do with it I couldn't even guess, but anyway she packed up and went thankfully back to the bright lights of the city. With equal thankfulness I returned to my normal wild and uncultured life on the farm. It was good to have my friend Miri reappear on the scene when the city girl left.

My friendship with Miri continued until Mother died and I was home alone with Father. She came often to visit me and would offer to help in the house if I was busy trying to rush the bread-baking or the washing through before it was time to go and help milk the cows. We understood each other well and were close friends.

Then one day I was shattered to find that a dress ring Father had given me for my birthday had disappeared. The ring was one his mother wore — I dared not tell him it had gone missing. The worst part of the whole sorry business was knowing perfectly well the ring hadn't just disappeared. It had been stolen. A ring can't get up and walk out of a closed trinket box.

I worried myself ill over the darned thing, knowing as I did that Miri was the only person who could possibly have taken it. She was the only one in the house when Father and I were at the milking sheds. I knew she admired the ring greatly.

Father and I went down to the river to visit a sick neighbour and stayed later than we had intended. I should have gone immediately we reached home to help Father with the milking but I was so dazzled by the flashing lights of a migraine headache I couldn't even see my way to the shed. So I crept onto my bed and lay there, trying not to breathe too deeply lest I jolted my wretched pounding head.

I heard Miri come into the kitchen and light the big wood-burning stove, and that worried me, too. Even after a couple of weeks I hadn't summoned the courage to accuse her of taking the ring. I knew I should do something about so valuable an heirloom, but I just could not face her with an accusation. She was like a sister to me.

I think she imagined I was down at the cowshed. She came

barging into my room without knocking — then there was a blank pause. I'd covered my aching eyes with a cool damp cloth but I sensed she was standing near the bed. "You've got a bad headache?" There was concern in her tone, but no note of guilt or apology.

I said something, I don't remember what. I had a sick feeling this was not the first time she had come uninvited into my room but I was in no state to take the question up with her just then.

She seemed to move round the room softly and I heard the blinds being drawn to shut out the late afternoon sun. Then she went out and closed the door. I must confess I looked the room over when I finally got up to make Father's evening meal but there seemed to be nothing missing. Much as I hated myself for my suspicions there could be little doubt that she knew her way about my room rather too well. She'd definitely been in there at some time during my absence from the house.

I opened my trinket box. The missing ring was back. She must have slipped it into the box while I lay there with closed eyes. There was nothing I could possibly think but that she'd become frightened and decided to return the ring she had stolen two weeks ago.

I'd never felt so bitterly disillusioned. I couldn't face her when I found her still in the kitchen. She asked if I were feeling better, then took something from the pocket of her jacket and held it out to me.

"From me to you," her pretty dark-skinned face beamed. "I got this ring for you because you are my friend."

It was a pretty little thing she had picked up at one of the local stores — Kaikohe, as it turned out. She'd ridden across country to get it, a two-hour ride each way over rough and trackless terrain.

I gaped at her. Surely she was not going to be stupid enough to make a peace offering? Nothing was going to alter the fact that she had taken my ring and returned it only because she'd panicked.

But then she added, "I took your other ring with me to get the right size. I didn't want you to know I'm getting this birthday present for you…"

It seemed ridiculous for anyone to suppose we'd had no opportunity to make close and loyal friends in the Hokianga. Visitors were always welcome at our place. There was a German professor of music, an alcoholic, long since dead and gone. His piano-playing was out of this world. We spent many delightful hours listening to his superb rendering of the classics.

We never did know where he came from, but he lived under Father's roof for some years, disappearing for long periods when the urge for alcohol became too strong for him. He didn't claim any relatives in New Zealand, poor old chap.

It must be ghastly to find oneself in a strange new land where no one really cares what fate overtakes you. We kids were horrified to learn that, although he did seem to believe in Gott in Himmel, he nevertheless had no faith in His good works.

All the same, we felt it must have been his Gott who led him to the shelter of Mother's and Father's unwavering hospitality and kindness. The Professor was a part of our young lives on the farm, we were really in awe of so gifted a musician.

Then there was the tiny, frail little mother of a famous Victoria Cross winner from the First World War. Mother nursed her back to health when she came to us in the peace and quiet of the country, her nerves shattered by the stress and unbearable tensions all wartime mothers suffer. Her frail delicate presence in our home did something for us robust young scallywags, rousing a protectiveness which never quite left us. Mother was the light of our lives and we adored her, but this tiny lady was something else again. Tiny or not, she must surely have passed on to her son the bravery which won him such acclaim.

I might mention the young fellow who simply could not or would not tell the truth. It was a psychological impossibility for him to do anything other than lie his head off even over the small happenings of everyday life. Issues that did not matter in the least to anyone. For instance, he would rush to the sheds and tell Father he was wanted on the phone. Father was naive in some ways and always swallowed the bait without question.

This thing seemed to go deeper than mere practical joking, the young man was so earnest about it all. You just had to believe him!

He'd turn up at the cowshed with the story of an approaching launch, the driver of which had phoned to say he wanted to see Father urgently at the riverside. Father would drop everything and rush to the wharf only to find there was no launch or anyone wishing to see him, urgently or otherwise. It must have been infuriating to Father to find out this was yet another of our guest's strange fabrications.

He was a quiet lad but seemed to be a great reader, constantly helping himself to books from our shelves and studying their contents for hours at a time. Then one day he took a book and sat down to read it. By chance we noticed he'd picked up the dictionary and moreover he was holding it upside down as he licked his finger and turned the pages at regular intervals.

As he returned the dictionary to the shelves he favoured us with his frank, ingenuous smile and said, "Sorry, I've read this book before, when I was in Australia. I didn't think much of the sad ending."

The poor fellow had been putting up a brave front, he obviously couldn't read a word. Or could he? We were left trying to puzzle out just how far his spoofing had gone. Was he fooling us when he pretended he could read, or when he appeared to be unable to distinguish one book from another?

We made friends with a variety of people from the gumlands. Men from every part of the world crossed our farm on their way out to the river where they hoped to be picked up by passing launches. Father invariably offered a cup of tea or mug of soup.

Life on the gumfields was pretty grim but no doubt the diggers counted it all worth while when they returned to their overseas homes with a small fortune to show for their efforts. We youngsters hung round hoping for a game of cricket or rounders before the visitors took off again, and sometimes they played cards or chess with us. We couldn't speak their language and they had only a smattering of ours but that made no difference to our friendship.

I wonder what they thought of us kids? Probably regarded us as a nest of young bush creatures untouched by civilisation as they knew it. There was not one of them who did not show appreciation of Mother's gentle English ways, her bright and ready wit. When they left New Zealand some of them banded together and sent us a parcel of pure silk embroidered handkerchiefs from some remote country — Hungary, I think it was. So they must have overlooked the innocent little pranks of a gaggle of young horrors.

How any parent could keep their sense of humour in Mother's circumstances Heaven only knows! Nine boisterous young brats — and a tenth who didn't quite make it into this world alive. A devoted husband who nevertheless never ceased to resent the colonial way of life and who blamed everyone except God for his misfortunes and the extent of his family. Not an easy man to live with, even Mother admitted this under stress.

So it was not altogether due to our religious upbringing I decided to cut out all this mother-of-nine business and become a nun. My closest friends at school were Roman Catholics and I admired them greatly. They seemed to know even more than we did what God was all about. I really felt dedicated enough to become a nun.

However, it didn't work out that way. I changed my mind and followed my sisters into the field of nursing, finding myself eventually on the nursing staff of the

Purposeful Methodist home missionary on wheels: Fred Sanderson in the 1930s

Coromandel hospital. I was hurrying back late for duty with a couple of friends also on the nursing staff when we spotted a fellow dressed in a dark suit and wearing a clerical 'dog collar.' He was coming towards us along the narrow footpath.

"It's the new parson," I muttered. "Spread out, kids, and give him the choice of taking a wild leap onto the road or falling into the ditch."

Little did I know I was light-heartedly thrusting into the town drain my future husband, who would become the father of my six children.

The next generation: Fred Sanderson, Noelene, Nora Sanderson and Ralph at the back; Martyn, Clif, Kelvin in the middle; David in front